PLACE OF FEAR

ATLANTIC ISLAND: GUARDIAN BOOK 2

RENNIE ST. JAMES

FREDRIC SHERNOFF

WHITEMARSH PRODUCTIONS, LLC

Scout Ainsley studied the plants and candles dotting the waiting room. The pale colors and soft music reminded him of a spa; however, he was in a psychiatrist's office. Dr. Avery Wake was the only counselor his parents required him to visit. As doctors went, she was the least annoying.

"You can go in now."

He didn't remember the receptionist's name, but he gave her a wide smile and tipped his chin down in a nod. "Thank you, ma'am."

Dr. Wake opened the door before he reached it. "Hi, Scout. It's good to see you. Come on in." The petite woman looked right for the part of psychiatrist. Her brown hair was pulled back in some type of bun and glasses perched on her nose. She typically nodded often when he spoke, but she also smiled which is more than the other doctors had done.

Taking his normal seat in the chair instead of the couch, Scout tilted his head and smirked. "You're just dying to ask me about it, aren't you?"

She laughed. "I must admit I've been curious since your parents said the FBI had questioned you on your eighteenth birthday. You know my love of action and spy movies."

Unlike the other therapists, she hadn't pushed him. Dr. Wake had shared parts of her life and interests before asking him questions. He winked at her even though he'd never been able to fluster her by flirting. "Yes, I do. It wasn't as dramatic as the movies make it look, but I was in an interrogation room."

"Joking aside, your parents also said it was a case of mistaken identity. There's nothing on your record, and there will be no follow-ups, correct?"

"Yes, mistaken identity." It was easier to agree with the lie than to share the truth that a time-traveling FBI agent had helped clear his name to repay a favor. That the favor was to an unknown person who could want Scout dead didn't help clarify the issue. He still struggled to understand everything that had happened on and after Atlantic Island.

"You know I won't require you to talk about this. However, I think you still need a friend like me. We all need to talk sometimes. It allows us to organize our thoughts and to get someone else's point of view." Notepad and pen in her lap, she held his gaze. "However, we all have secrets and that's okay too."

It was Leyna's secrets that were bothering Scout though he had plenty of his own. He hadn't confessed to anyone other than Leyna about the voices in his head. Leyna didn't know how strongly he felt the connection to the Mayan artifacts or how his nightmares had changed. She didn't know he might need to walk through the Underworld. The words started flowing as his heart raced. "There is something I want to talk about if that's okay. Did my parents also tell you about Leyna? My…girlfriend."

"Yes, but I'm glad you brought up Ms. Carlyn. How are things going with her?"

"She lied to me." Scout stood to pace the room. Dr. Wake didn't get nervous at his need to move as the other doctors had. "Leyna is different. She's not at all like the friends I once had before the Island. I don't know that we would've gotten along if I'd met her then."

"But you met her after the Island." Dr. Wake was also the only one who didn't insist on adding the word "hallucination" when discussing his past.

"Yes, and I fell hard for her. She made me feel normal and sane. She made me smile and wish for a happy future."

"That's great, but remember we talked about your strength coming from inside you. A support system is wonderful. Your happiness and progress are because of you. Give yourself some credit for how far you've come."

Pausing to look out the window, Scout nodded to his reflection. His hair was short and he'd shaved that morning after working out. It still required effort, but he looked normal. "It's been a journey I never thought I'd have to make. Life was perfectly mapped out before the Island. I'm on track with those goals." He spun around in his rush to reassure her.

Dr. Wake smiled and pointed to a folder. "I get updates from your parents and school. Your grades are good, and it's looking like you'll be captain of the tennis team again. You've been applying to colleges too. You don't have to convince me."

"Thank you for that." He took a deep breath and

returned his attention to the outside world. It wasn't easy to ignore his image in the window, but he tried.

"Scout, why don't you tell me more about Leyna?"

He didn't pace, but he did stare at his reflection. Lies had become much easier after Atlantic Island. In Dr. Wake's office, he tried to speak the truth even if it required metaphors. She was more liberal than the other head shrinks, but it would be pushing his luck to talk about magical artifacts, time travel, and superhero powers. Scout closed his eyes and tried to remember the words he'd practiced in his head.

"Like I said, Leyna is different, but we are good together." He bit back the word *partner* since it tasted sour on his tongue. "We have the same goals and enjoy being together. It was perfect. Too perfect really, and it wasn't true."

"Nothing in this world is truly perfect. Moments and people can be perfect for us. Does that make sense, Scout?"

"It does, but that's not what I meant. I found out she lied to me. It's not something I want to share with you." He turned to give her a half-hearted shrug and wide eyes.

"You don't have to share everything. It does help if I know enough to be able to offer advice."

He had suspected she wouldn't be so easily deterred. Scout turned back to the window and sighed. "A friend" -using the word to describe Hodges' supporter, Gerard, almost choked him- "told me she had lied about her past. Another friend verified that." The FBI wasn't truly his friend either. It didn't improve his mood to realize he didn't really have any friends.

"Did you ask Leyna about it?"

Dr. Wake's voice was always calm and well-modulated. Scout leaned his head against the cool window and let it soothe the hot edges of the anger he hadn't been able to shake. It had been over a week since the Turtle had saved his life – over a week since he had denied both Hodges' rogue agents and Thomas' Multiversal Monitoring and Enforcement Agency – over a week since he'd started lying to Leyna.

"Scout? Would you like a glass of water? Tea perhaps?"

Lifting his head, he ignored the last questions to return to the first one. "I want to talk to Leyna about it, but I haven't. Why would she tell me the truth now?"

The doctor didn't answer immediately and typically that was something he appreciated. She often acted as a sounding board while the other doctors had talked more than they had listened. He needed answers this time. Scout needed to know whom to trust and what to do. Following the voices in his head had given him two artifacts. They'd also brought Leyna into his life. He couldn't trust Thomas or Gerard, but he wasn't sure he could trust himself either. "What if I'm not strong enough? What if I'm broken?"

"It's okay to have doubts about others and ourselves. Is there a specific task that concerns you or is this a general worry for the future?"

He hadn't meant to ask the questions hiding in the darkness of his head and heart. Scout wasn't sure he wanted those answers. The Jaguar had brought him strength, and the Turtle had healed his injuries, but the fear and doubt remained. He wasn't sure it was enough...he wasn't sure *he* was enough. The expectations had changed, but there were adults in his life who were still trying to map out his life for him. Everyone expected him to find and understand all four artifacts. Scout couldn't see a bright future anymore; he saw only shadows.

"Did you hear me? I'd like to talk about this." Dr. Wake stood close enough for her reflection to join his in the window.

Scout flinched and jerked away. He took several steps back before turning to face her. "What do you think dreams mean?"

If she was thrown by the abrupt subject change, she didn't show it. Dr. Wake resumed her seat and then met his gaze. "We still understand very little about the human brain. Freud believed dreams show hidden desires. Research suggests dreams may help us process intense emotions or catalog our memories. Unfortunately, I don't know the latest studies, but I'll look some up for you."

"What do *you* think they mean?" Scout stepped closer to press for an answer.

Dr. Wake shook her head. "What matters is what you believe they mean."

Mumbling a curse, he turned away again. His reflection revealed the frown and clenched jaw. He tried to relax, but memories of his recent dreams filled his mind with snakes, jaguars, and blood. "I think they reveal what we fear."

New words had joined the mantra in this head whether he was asleep or awake.

Xibalba...place of fear...

"Scout, what do you fear?" Dr. Wake placed her pen on the pad and clasped her hands together as she waited.

He couldn't find the truth to share or hide from her. The voices were silent in his head and he could only see shadows.

"It's okay. We can talk about this more or we can talk

about something else." She paused then made the decision for him. "How is Maya's training going?"

The remainder of the session was lighter and Scout smiled at the receptionist when he left. He couldn't shake the feeling of the darkness following him.

2

Scout kept his smile in place as he crammed his jacket in his locker. Leyna Carlyn slid into place next to him and reached one hand out. She'd developed the new habit of placing her hand over his heart. There was barely a faint scar marking the injury that should've ended his life. After battling both the MMEA and rogue agents in Mexico, Leyna had Traveled them back to Virginia. She'd thought he was dying. The Mayan Turtle had healed him; it had saved him. He couldn't help but wonder if she had reported that fact to Thomas—neither the MMEA leader nor Gerard had approached him again.

"Morning." Leyna left the hand on his heart as she pressed a kiss to his lips.

"Morning, Sunshine," Scout teased before edging back a mere inch. It was still difficult to reconcile her appearance with what he now knew about her. It was easier to see the troubled Salem witch saved by Marcus than the Multiversal Monitoring and Enforcement Agency plant following Thomas' orders. Leyna still favored all black clothes, kept her dark hair pixie short, and constantly changed her various piercings. He tried not to dwell on the strong, petite body hovering close enough for him to feel her warmth.

Students rushed through the hallway even as he and Leyna remained still. Scout almost asked why she continued the ploy of school, but he was sure he knew the answer. Her MMEA job was to watch him, and she had to stick close to do that well. He forced his clenched hands to open and tried to focus on her words.

"I haven't received any more messages from Brenley. Maybe we should pop back down there to visit her and Dacey. No one is going to leave us alone, and we still need answers."

"I guess an archeologist and an artist might be our best source of information." He nodded, but more for confirmation of his thoughts. As Gerard had warned, Leyna was always pushing to advance the artifacts search. Scout's smile for the principal was welcoming—the interruption of the conversation was appreciated.

"Ms. Carlyn, Mr. Ainsley, I see the two of you in the hallway quite often. Don't you have classes?"

"Yes, sir." Scout didn't realize he'd moved to stand at attention until he noted Leyna rolling her eyes. The soldier habits learned on Atlantic Island had refused to be forgotten.

"Then get moving," Mr. Richmond directed.

Nodding to the man, Scout met Leyna's eyes for a brief second before making his escape. He could feel her eyes on his back, but he knew she wouldn't risk blowing her cover by disobeying their principal. Sliding into his seat, he tried to slow his breathing and his racing heart. The nightmarish images of jaguars and snakes flared brightly in his mind. It wasn't only his vision he lost control of whenever his heart raced. He could smell salt, blood, and something he couldn't identify. It reminded him of pine and something else. Since the Turtle had saved him—

"Mr. Ainsley?"

Blinking, Scout met his teacher's gaze as a few students snickered. "I'm sorry, ma'am …um, what?"

Ms. Brown shook her head and pointed back to the screen. "Studying constellations tells us about our world scientifically, but it's more than just hard science. I'm not talking about astrology—"

"Hey baby, what's your sign?"

The class erupted into laughter at the bad pick-up line. Scout felt his breath ease out in a chuckle too. He opened his tablet to follow along and embrace the distraction.

"Constellations have been studied by humans throughout history. Whether it's the Egyptian pyramids or Stonehenge, historians believe people have used the night sky to inspire science, religion, and art. I know our syllabus calls for a trip, but that has been canceled. I still want us to explore some other views of the stars." Ms. Brown tapped her laptop to change the screen then pressed a few more buttons.

Scout blinked as he received the updated materials—his eyes couldn't look past one word.

"These podcasts explore some of the ancient views of the constellations and the mythology around them. I've coordinated with both Ms. Davis and Mr. Wade so your papers will be counted in their classes too."

The teacher droned on about the specifics as Scout continued to stare at his screen.

"…Mayans." Ms. Brown smiled and nodded at the class. "You have two weeks to complete the paper. Don't forget to cite your sources. Now, let's get back to the scientific theories and discoveries surrounding the constellations."

"The celestial sphere is divided into eighty-eight sections. Not every star is in a constellation; however, they are in a section. While different cultures gave different names to the same stars, we now use coordinates…"

Scout tried to follow along, but he kept clicking back to the podcast dedicated to the Mayans. He knew the hunter Orion was represented by a turtle since that was what led them to Dacey and the artifact. He hadn't thought to see if there were correlations for the Owl and Snake. Tapping a finger, he resisted the impulse to start his new research immediately.

He wasn't able to stop himself from contacting Dr. Brenley Golnar. The archeologist had already proven to be invaluable with her knowledge of Mayan history and culture. Without any knowledge of time travel, she was also someone neither side claimed though both had used her. Scout couldn't stop a wince and his fingers stilled on the keyboard; he was also using the doctor. Pushing aside the guilt, he focused on the job and completed the message. Brenley was one of the few people without an agenda, and he trusted her.

There was no response from Brenley though Scout checked his phone repeatedly. He stayed late after two afternoon classes to avoid Leyna. It was easier to think clearly without her nearby. Tennis practice gave him an outlet for his anger and allowed another chance to delay seeing his 'partner'. But he couldn't delay the inevitable as they trained together most evenings.

"Hey, stranger." Leyna sat on the folded blanket with her back against a tree.

"Hey back." He offered her a hand and didn't stop her from slamming into him for an open-mouthed kiss. "Ready to train?"

"Right to business, huh? I thought maybe we could chat." She paused and held his gaze for several seconds. "Are you doing okay? Do you think there are lingering effects from the Turtle healing you?"

He looked away but stood still when her hand landed above his heart. "I told you I'm fine. We may never know the exact impact of the artifacts. Didn't we decide to limit our use of them for that reason? I've hidden both away and change the locations often."

Leyna's fingers tapped against his shirt, and Scout's heart rate accelerated. The world blurred at the edges of his vision until he struggled to breathe calmly. He spun away and sought a distraction for them both. "The ceiba tree stands strong against the winds of time and isn't broken by the powers hidden in the darkness; waves of pain will drown the unworthy and fire from the sky will burn any who seek to cut down the tree."

"Is that—"

"The curse, yes. Brenley told us about it." Scout looked back to see her frown.

"You memorized it? How? Why?"

His mistake was obvious now, and Scout scrambled to find an acceptable mix of truth and lies. "I gave Brenley my number and we've talked some. I needed to know her translation of the curse so I can ask Dacey about it."

The frown slowly smoothed out, but Leyna didn't smile. "Oh, that makes sense. I didn't realize you two spoke directly. I thought we were using the website."

"We were, we are. Both Hodges' agents and the MMEA know about her so I didn't think it would hurt to ask. I thought I had an idea and needed her help, but that didn't pan out." Scout tried to stop rambling. "We'll keep using the website as that won't look suspicious to anyone."

"What do you want to train on today?" Leyna scratched her nose then twisted one earring several times. Her gaze flitted around the forest.

Scout stepped closer then stopped and clenched his fists. He wasn't sure if she was upset because she didn't like Brenley or because she didn't have access to more information for Thomas. He also wasn't sure if he wanted to comfort her or call her out on her lies. "Why don't we do a little hand-to-hand then sprint the escape routes?"

They followed some of the drills commanders had shown them on Atlantic Island. He'd learned the series of open-handed strikes and blocks as knife katas. Most of his training had involved weapons of some kind, but desperation had been part of daily life there. It hadn't always been about causes or politics. Sometimes, it was simply about food and survival. He forced the memories back before panic could take hold again. His distraction did allow Leyna to land a few additional strikes.

"Nice." Scout dragged in a little more air and backed off.

"I believe you taught me that move." Leyna laughed before spinning away. She tossed him a bottle of water and kept one for herself.

After a quick drink, he dropped it to the ground. "Let's go again then we'll run."

Determined, he varied the speed of the familiar movements. Leyna frowned and missed one block after moving too fast. She glared at him but kept going. Scout waited for only one additional second before striking out of order and stepped closer to her. Their movements were chaotic during the freestyle drill.

Low block – forward kick – throat punch – heel strike.

Dodge – thrust – pivot.

He pushed Leyna's shoulder hard enough to send her falling back then sprinted away. Scout opened his senses as he ran. Controlling his breathing, he couldn't detect the salty air or blood that coated his dreams. The smell of pine was surprisingly comforting. Leyna's rapid steps grew louder as she chased him. When she veered to take another route, he plowed forward. Scout reached the bridge before her but slammed to a stop when an elderly woman walking her dog blocked his path. The small fluffy animal yapped and charged toward him.

"No, Roscoe. Be a good boy."

Scout didn't hear Leyna until she sprinted through the small stream with a laugh.

"You really should follow your girlfriend, young man."

Biting back a retort, Scout nodded to the stranger. "Yes, ma'am."

3

THE NEXT DAYS AND NIGHTS PASSED IN A BLUR OF SCHOOL, tennis, Leyna, research, and nightmares. Scout was still waiting for Thomas or Gerard to ambush him with another request or deal. There was a part of him that worried either or both could target his family instead. Stepping inside the front door, he paused to listen even as he picked up the wriggling dog at his feet.

"Hi, Maya." Scout tucked the animal in close to quiet her happy barks. "Just give me a minute. Stay quiet."

There were no signs his parents were in the house, nor any other presence. Scout released a shaky breath and hugged the dog closer. "Okay, girl, we'll go out now."

It was another part of his daily routine. Each morning and evening, he and Maya would train in the back yard. It was nothing fancy, just a routine of squats, lunges, bear crawls, and pull-ups. He had managed to create a hidden parkour course in the spacious area. Unfortunately, he'd already had to replace one decorative lantern when he had misjudged the distance across the table. His leap didn't clear the light – he and it had tumbled to the ground.

When Maya barked, Scout laughed and took the hint. He grabbed a towel to wipe the sweat from his face before gathering her toys. He'd researched dog obstacle courses and had even sold his parents on the need for them...as long as he kept the mess stowed in the storage building when not in use.

The small balance beam, hoop, and bright red tunnels gave him and Maya new training experiences. He altered the setup to work them both.

"Wait, Maya."

Her whole body shivered, but she remained by his side. "Tunnels."

She sprinted across the yard with him behind her. While she easily ran through, he was forced to belly crawl. She came around a second then a third time before he finished.

Without giving her a command, he jumped over the tunnel and crossed the beam he'd placed only a couple of feet off the ground. She followed without making a sound. He stepped off it then reached into his pocket for the small toy. As soon as he launched it across the yard, she took off. He jumped rope for the minute and a half it took her to retrieve the ball, run the course, and return it to him.

"Go!" Scout pointed to the hoop hanging a foot off the ground.

In a blur of light brown fur, she ran and leapt through it. He dove through the hoop and landed in a roll. His right shoulder jammed into the ground, but he was able to stand. He tossed the ball with his left hand then rubbed his shoulder.

Maya again returned to drop the ball at his feet. They

continued with several more throws until Scout heard the back door open.

"There you are." His mom stepped out of the house with a smile for them. "They don't have courses like this at Westminster, do they?"

Scout couldn't help but laugh. His parents would've preferred buying a purebred, but he had fallen in love with the muddy stray he'd first met in the park. "No, they don't. You want to watch her really move fast?"

She smiled and sighed. "Of course. Please do allow your little dog to demonstrate her skills."

After studying how owners communicated with deaf dogs, Scout had started using hand signals mixed with verbal commands for Maya. It was fascinating how much deaf dogs could learn and understand, and he enjoyed challenging his pup. He didn't truly believe his enemies would target her, but she was his responsibility.

Without saying a word, he directed Maya toward the tunnel. He jogged along with her as he led her through the course and had her walk on her hind legs. His mom's laughter made him smile and Maya bark. After a few more stunts, they both skidded to a stop next to his mom.

"Maya, you are indeed a very talented girl." She patted the dog's head lightly then turned to kiss Scout's cheek. "You were right when you said she was good therapy for you. It's nice to see you playing with her."

"I'm sorry – did you say I was right?" He pretended to hit his ear before tilting his head from side to side.

His mother matched his height in her heels, but she somehow managed to look down on him with a pointed look. "Now, your father will be home soon so please put away that mess and come inside. If it takes more than five minutes, put your jacket back on. It's still winter and you could get sick."

"Yes, ma'am." Scout tipped an imaginary hat, which made his mom laugh.

She stopped by the door to face him again. Her smile was soft. "I'm very glad Maya joined our family. I'd missed your smile. You smile a lot when you play with your dog."

Scout could only nod and stare at the door that closed behind her. Her words bounced around his head as he tried to process them. Training was a means of survival, it wasn't play. His mom wasn't wrong though. He did enjoy it...he enjoyed training as a soldier should.

Even with the pleasantly exhausted feeling lingering after a hot shower, Scout dreaded going to bed. He put it off as long as possible by continuing his research on the constellations. Brenley had yet to answer his request for information. He'd already listened to the Mayan astronomy podcast several times and had started a new document of notes on the Mayan view of the sky. Resting on the bed, he pulled up the document and gave Maya's ears a scratch.

"We know the Pleiades constellation was drawn as a rattlesnake. Of course, that doesn't tell us where the Snake artifact could be or how we can find it."

Switching to another screen, he studied the cluster of stars. "I don't see anything in that but random dots." He zoomed out until he could see the three stars that created Orion's belt.

"Maya, in Greek mythology, Orion is chasing the Seven Sisters, the Pleiades, across the heavens. That works well for the hunter thing, but I don't understand the connection between the Turtle and the Snake that we need to find."

He moved back to his research notes to review them again. Maya cuddled close and he petted her with one hand. Occasionally, he muttered a few words out loud.

"Rainy season."

After a quick break for dog cuddles, he returned to his research.

"There is a possible connection to the Jaguar if those scholars were right."

His eyes were burning, but he kept reading through several more pages.

"Quetzalcóatl or Kukulkan."

Scout didn't recall falling asleep. The nightmares hit him hard and fast. It always started with the cenote.

Salty air coated his skin just as blood soaked the rocks at his feet. The voices were silent, but he didn't need to hear the word. He understood where he was and he was afraid.

Xibalba.

The Underworld.

His heart raced as he waited for the jaguar and snake. The sound of claws scratching the rocks behind him caused his body to tremble. Scout felt the warm breath hit his neck just as a rattling noise shook the ground.

He tried to wake up as he usually did, but instead, he felt raindrops land on his skin. Looking up, the night sky was visible through the cave's opening. Orion stood poised behind the Seven Sisters. Lightning flashed red instead of white and pain lanced through Scout's body. His knees scraped along the rocks, burning and aching, after his fall to the ground. Snake eyes stared at him— red and pulsing. A forked tongue flicked against his face.

Scout reached out a hand to protect himself as he tried to scramble back. There was no ground behind him. He fell into the darkness…and kept falling.

Opening his eyes, he saw Maya on the edge of the bed above him. Scout huffed out a laugh and wiped the wetness from his face. The dog jumped down and licked his cheek again.

"Thanks for pulling me from that nightmare, girl."

4

"Brenley?" Scout scrubbed a hand across his face and sat up in the bed. The archeologist's words finally penetrated the sleepy haze.

"...Dacey is gone. The house is empty. He isn't responding to my calls or messages." Panic brought a sharp edge to her normally calm tone.

"Back up, Doc. When was the last time you saw him?"

"Just after you did. We spent that night together, but then he was gone. I didn't think anything of it at first."

Scout scratched Maya's ears and waited. He could hear the deep gulping breaths on the other end of the line as the woman struggled for control. It took him a moment to realize he was counting in his head as if he was the one having a panic attack.

"Dacey goes off on his own often, and I get lost in my work. It's not like we talk daily. I didn't notice." Her voice cracked then there was silence for several seconds before she continued in a quiet, firm voice. "I need your help, Scout. I think something horrible has happened to him."

"Okay. I mean, yes, of course. I'll help you." He stood and ran through options in his head. As Dacey was connected to the artifacts, both sides would be interested in him. Either one could've taken him. War meant collateral damage and even the FBI agent had warned him about that. Dacey could've been an easier target than Scout—

"Thank you. I'll buy your plane tickets and send the details…"

Scout's laughter drowned out Brenley's words. "That won't be necessary. We'll be there much sooner than you'd think possible. It's seven o'clock in the morning here now. You'll see us soon."

"Us? Leyna will join you?"

Shrugging, he was glad she couldn't see his expression. He couldn't entirely blame Leyna without blaming himself as he was still using her as his time taxi. "Yeah, Leyna will definitely be with me. After we find Dacey, we probably all owe you some explanations."

"Fine, I will see you both when you get here. I'm at my tent." The familiar cadence was back in her voice as she regained control.

"We'll see ya soon." Scout wasn't sure she waited long enough to hear his words. Tossing the phone on the bed, he rushed through his shower and returned quickly. He reviewed his notes on Dacey and continued to count his breaths in his head. Maya sat on the floor pouting.

"Sorry, girl. No time for a morning workout today. I promise I'll make time for us to do a double tonight." He shook his head and tried not to think about time, time travel, or Leyna. He couldn't ignore Leyna or his need for her.

He grabbed his phone and sent her a message—*You ready to travel today? Heard from Doc.*

Pulling the artifacts from the most recent hiding place, he paused and took a deep breath. The voices and images in his head were connected to them, to the orb. Scout still didn't understand how, but he understood the rush of power he felt whenever he held them. "If Dacey has been captured by Thomas or Hodges, we're gonna need all the power we can get."

He left them wrapped and stuffed both into his bag. Warmth still raced through his body; bright images of the sun, fire, and water flared in his mind. His muscles quivered as he tried to suppress the need to move, the desire for fight or flight.

"Be a good girl, Maya. I'll be back as soon as I can." Scout paused and met the dog's brown eyes. "I will be back."

Sprinting from the house, Scout managed to avoid his parents. He'd barely glanced at Leyna's response to his message; there was no time to answer her questions. There was also the fact that he preferred to leave few data trails, and he wanted to see her face when he shared the latest news.

The hallways were crowded with students dragging to their first classes. Scout eased through the masses to stop by his locker for chocolate. He wasn't surprised to see Leyna already pacing the library media workroom they always used.

"What's going on? Your message only—"

"There wasn't time to explain everything. Brenley called me early this morning. She said Dacey has disappeared. She hasn't seen him since we got the Turtle and he's not responding to her calls or messages. We led the MMEA and Hodges' guys straight to Dacey, and he would have been an easy target. They could've taken him. We need—"

"No, Thomas wouldn't do that," Leyna interrupted. She turned away shaking her head repeatedly. "It has to be Hodges' supporters. They are the rogue agents. It's not Thomas; it can't be him."

Scout waited until she turned back and met his gaze. "Okay. We need to see if we can find Dacey regardless of who took him. We don't technically know anyone did. It's suspicious that he's completely disappeared just after giving me the Turtle."

She didn't seem to appreciate the easy victory and wasn't ready to change the subject. "I know you don't fully trust Thomas, but you have to see he's doing what's right. He's fighting to save the Universe."

"Yeah, I get that, and I get that war is hell."

"Scout, I'm sorry." Leyna latched on to his hands. "I know Atlantic Island was hell for you. This is different though. Thomas saved the Island, and he's going to save the Universe. You aren't crazy. You are definitely not alone. We're partners."

He brushed a kiss across her mouth but didn't linger. "I know, and I am glad you're here. I even brought extra chocolate."

She laughed and took the candy. "Where are we going and when?"

"Brenley said she was at her tent when we talked and that was seven o'clock this morning. I say we go to her tent now." He pulled out clothes and avoided looking at Leyna.

"That's barely an hour. She's not going to believe we flew in."

Turning back as he stripped off his long-sleeved shirt to leave him in a tee-shirt, Scout nodded. "I think I have to tell her the truth. She's seen a lot already and now with Dacey."

"It's not only whether she deserves the truth." Grabbing his arm, Leyna frowned at him with shiny eyes. "Scout, it's also about whether she can accept it and what she'll do with that knowledge."

Scout looked away from the possibility of her tears. "I'm sure your family—"

"This isn't about me," Leyna spoke over him again.

"Brenley can handle this. She won't take action against us. If she'd wanted to do that, she would've helped the FBI put me in jail. She's not involved in the MMEA battle. She's not a Traveler. She's an academic. She won't freak out, and I'm going to tell her."

"And what if she wants to go back to the Mayan civilization to satisfy her academic curiosity? What happens then?" Hands on her hips, Leyna stood directly in front of him.

He shrugged to acknowledge her point. "Yeah, she'll be curious, but she's too smart to want to mess up history."

"I'm not taking her anywhere."

"Fair enough," Scout conceded. He finished dressing as Leyna started. His thoughts pulled him in a million directions, but his eyes were glued to the partner he had to trust with his life. "You ready?"

She stepped close and wrapped her arms around his waist. "Let's do this."

5

PUSHING THROUGH THE TENT FLAP, SCOUT FROZE BEFORE snapping his mouth shut. Leyna bumped into him with a groan. Brenley's head jerked up to stare at them. The red eyes and tear stains made him swallow around the lump in his throat. Leyna shuffled behind him without speaking.

The archeologist stood as she wiped both hands over her face. Her smile faltered and she stared at her watch. "We spoke an hour ago, but you're here now."

"Yes." Scout didn't blink or offer an explanation. When Brenley nodded, he smiled. "There are some things we're gonna have to talk about later, Doc. For now, let's see if we can find Dacey."

She glanced at her watch then dabbed at her eyes. "Yes, let's find Dacey. I'm not sure what I think you can do, but..."

When Brenley didn't finish the sentence, Scout laughed. "I'm not sure either. We're still gonna try. You've helped me and so has Dacey. The least I can do is try to help you."

An awkward silence fell. Scout shifted the pack on his back and imagined he could feel the Turtle Dacey had held. Brow furrowed, Brenley lowered her gaze to her watch again. The tapping of the pen against her leg counted the seconds.

"Why don't we go to his house? You can go through the details again with both of us."

Scout was grateful for Leyna's business approach and nodded. The plan pulled Brenley out of her thoughts too.

"Yes, that was the last place I saw him. The police here won't help. I don't want to contact U.S. authorities after that FBI issue." A red flush rose over Brenley's face, but she stared at Scout. "I do not understand what's going on. Everything points back to you."

"That seems to be the general consensus right now," Scout grumbled. He forced a smile when both Leyna and Brenley flinched. "Look, I don't have the answers. We worked well together previously, and we still have the same goal. We want the truth. That counts for something, doesn't it?"

Slamming her laptop closed, Brenley placed it in her bag. "It does, and it's all I have right now."

"Let's go then." Leyna held the flap open and gestured for them to lead.

Scout stopped next to Brenley as she stared at the rising sun. She turned to meet his eyes.

"The directions were something you asked about earlier. The parchment had the four directions and four animals."

"Yes," Scout confirmed when the archeologist paused.

"One animal was a turtle. Dacey gave you a turtle statue. He said it belonged in his family, but was yours."

He frowned at that new information, but she continued before he could ask any questions.

"You both acted strangely that day. Although, I've never known either of you to be normal, which nullifies such conclusions."

Leyna sniffed behind him as Scout grinned. He couldn't help teasing the doctor. "The world is just one big experiment for you, isn't it?"

"How else should one live if not to learn?" Brenley resumed walking through the empty field. "We don't have time to discuss these things."

While Brenley marched ahead, Leyna moved next to Scout and tugged his arm for him to walk slower. "Still want to tell her the truth?"

"Yes." Scout studied the rising sun once more as images played in his head. Jaguar, Turtle, Snake, and Owl. South, West, East, and North. Xibalba. He'd been terrified when he'd thought he was alone; now, he worried about those around him.

"You okay?" Leyna stopped walking and shielded her eyes to study him.

He briefly met her gaze before looking in each direction. He ignored the fear and turned back to Leyna. "We have work to do."

Without waiting for a response, he jogged toward Brenley. The sound of Leyna's footsteps behind him brought a rush of adrenaline. Scout sped up and rejoined the archeologist before she made it to her vehicle.

Brenley didn't play any music, nor did she speak as she drove. Scout refused to glance at Leyna in the back seat, but he could hear the creak of her seat each time she shifted. He let his thoughts return to Dacey. Memories from their one and only meeting flitted through his mind. The artist had been different. Scout almost laughed at the thought of judging anyone else on his skewed normal curve. At least, Dacey hadn't been involved in the showdown between Gerard's men and Thomas' agents. He tried to focus on the minutes before that when they'd been with Dacey. Brenley's voice pulled Scout from the memories.

"That last night with Dacey is a bit of a blur. I remember you two leaving then I remember us having dinner."

"Wait, you don't remember the..." Leyna looked at Scout without finishing her question.

"Remember what?"

"I fell into the scrap metal pile. It probably made a lot of noise." Scout shot a look to keep Leyna quiet before giving Brenley a small grin. "Leyna and I were goofing off and I lost."

Brenley took several seconds to reply. "No, I don't remember that."

Rolling her eyes, Leyna shifted on her seat. "What do you remember exactly?"

"I didn't lie. Dacey has always been different, and he said the same thing about me. He said it with awe instead of amusement though." The archeologist kept her gaze on the road, but her hands tightened on the steering wheel. "When I study history, I feel like I'm there. It's part of me and I'm part of it. Dacey saw the Mayans the same way. We've worked together for a couple of years. It wasn't the first time I'd stayed at his house."

Again, pink spread across her face, and panic returned to her voice. Scout couldn't look away from her.

"If I'd known it would be the last time..."

"Hey, don't do that." Scout pried one hand off the steering wheel and held it. He squeezed gently until she glanced at him. "Let's see what we can find out before we give up, okay?"

"You don't understand." Brenley pulled her hand away and wiped away new tears. "I can't remember those other nights. I just know it wasn't the first one."

Leyna's gasp filled the silence. "You can't remember him?"

"I can't explain it, but the memories are hazy. I feel like my eyes are tired and I need to blink to clear my vision. It doesn't help. They continue to fade away."

"That doesn't make sense—" Leyna didn't get any further.

"You don't think I know that? The human brain doesn't work like that. The memories shouldn't disappear overnight without a traumatic event, and certainly not the memories of one man. It doesn't make sense. None of this makes sense." Brenley's voice grew louder and higher pitched. The silence that fell was deafening.

Scout stared out his window and counted his breaths in his head. It sounded too much like Dacey's life was being erased. The words of the FBI agent repeated in his head. *You screw up again and they'll erase your existence from the multiverse.*

"I really don't know what you can do, but I appreciate you trying." Brenley got out and slammed the door behind her.

Blinking, Scout realized they were parked in front of Dacey's house. His thoughts swirled as he reached for his bag.

"Scout, this isn't normal. If Hodges' agents did something, they are probably watching his house right now. You need to be careful."

"Yeah." He reached blindly into his bag as he studied the house and yard. The flare of heat in his fingers confirmed he'd found the Jaguar. Scout took a deep breath and let the energy flow through him. The lighter pulses of the Turtle joined the flow with a cooler burst. "Stay close to me and Brenley in case we need to make a speedy departure."

6

BRACING HIS LEGS A LITTLE WIDER APART, SCOUT SHIELDED his eyes and scanned the back yard. There was no sign of danger or that there had been any trouble. The front yard had been equally cleared of any evidence, even of their fight with the MMEA and Gerard. He barely spared a glance for the pile of scrap metal, but Leyna had glared at it for a full minute.

"Can you get us inside?" Scout turned to the archeologist when she didn't immediately reply. She stood frozen, staring at the house with wide eyes. He placed a hand on the small of her back. "Brenley, do you have a key?"

Her shoulders jerked back before she looked at him. "Yes, let's go inside."

Scout pushed by her to enter first. "You two stay out here for a second. I want to test out a theory."

Neither woman looked happy, but neither argued.

He stepped inside the artist's house. Open and airy, Dacey's art and tools were the primary decoration. Scout had vivid memories of his first visit and little had changed. There was no obvious evidence of foul play. It looked like Dacey had just stepped outside. Taking a deep breath, he focused on the memory of his first visit.

Even before his near-death experience, things had been weird. He had been shocked by Dacey's offer that he could have the Turtle if he could find it. It was no less shocking to Scout that he'd been able to find it. The strange twists had kept coming. Only Dacey had felt the tremors signaling the presence of Hodges' and Thomas' forces. He'd also seemed to understand more than Scout did about the dangers. The artist was as mysterious as the artifacts – Scout had hoped Dacey would become an ally.

Pulling back from the past, he dug inside the bag again. He ignored the Jaguar in favor of the Turtle. After unwrapping it, he held it in his hands and closed his eyes. There were no images, voices, or earthquakes; there was no Dacey either. He opened one eye then the other, but nothing had changed. "That's a little anticlimactic."

The women entered the room before he could continue his private conversation.

"What are you doing?" Leyna strode forward to stand next to him.

"I'm trying to see if I can find any clues about Dacey." Scout wanted to apologize to Brenley, but Leyna grabbed his arm. Her frown was more wary than angry.

"Clues about what?"

Brenley's face paled. "I can only remember the last night with him."

"With who?"

Scout looked from one to the other, hoping it was some elaborate prank. Tears were forming in Brenley's eyes so he turned to Leyna. "Dacey Cadmael. The artist who had the Turtle? Tall guy, dark hair. Expert on Mayan art who worked with Brenley. Seriously, you don't remember being here with him?"

Leyna peered up at him. "Are you feeling okay? Did you have another incident?" She glanced at Brenley as she stumbled over the last word. Her next words were too low for the archaeologist to hear. "Did the voices tell you about Dacey?"

A flash of heat almost made him drop the Turtle. Tightening his grip, he turned away from both of them. "Please stay here. I'll be right back."

Breathing deeply, Scout hoped the artifact could guide him again. If he didn't focus on the strangeness of the newest issues, he might not panic or overthink. He pictured Maya with her pink tongue and floppy ear. His breathing steadied and made it easier to remember Dacey. Scout's feet carried him out of the house and through the back yard. The rising sun already brought warmth, but it paled in comparison to the energy flooding his body. He studied the waves blurring the desert landscape ahead. Rushing forward, he skidded in the sand as his legs stopped moving.

Scout glanced around as more warmth flooded his body. He crouched down and brushed away the sand. The rocks below were polished smooth and painted a rich, sandy red. The heat of the stone almost burned his hands when he swept back more dirt. A familiar image carved into the stone was fully revealed: Orion hunting the Seven Sisters.

A quick glance proved he was still alone. Scout placed the Turtle on Orion then placed his free hand on the Pleiades. He again closed his eyes and tried to breathe calmly. His first attempt had failed but—

"Xibalba."

Scout fell back on his butt and stared at Dacey. The

man shimmered as if he were a desert mirage. Blinking didn't bring him into focus. "Dacey? Are you okay? Where have you been?"

The man grinned before he stared past Scout. "You shouldn't have brought her. She shouldn't remember me."

"Wait, you know she can't remember you? Leyna can't either. What's going on? Who wiped their memories? How did they even do that? Why did they do it?" Scout stuttered through the questions. Several more tumbled in his head and gave him a headache. He rubbed at the back of his neck then grimaced at the sweat covering his hand. A part of him expected Dacey to be gone when he looked up again, but the artist stood a few feet away and glared at him.

"I told you the Turtle was your responsibility. You need to find the others before they do."

"Sure, you make it sound easy."

Dacey ignored his interruption. "It's your duty as the Guardian. No one else can do it."

"Right now, we are trying to find *you*," Scout retorted. He clambered to his feet and stretched out a hand without reaching the other man.

"This isn't about me. It's your time. Use your connection to the Turtle and Jaguar to direct you to the Snake then the Owl. Balance, guide, and protect."

The man's image shivered as the ground shook. Scout regained his balance and looked up in time to see Dacey fade into nothing. He reached out but found only air. Biting back a curse, he dropped to a knee and picked up the Turtle. It was cool to the touch once again. The rock was also cold, but now a long crack split the space between Orion and the Sisters. Scout used one finger to trace it. Dacey was gone and the voices silent, but he still had no idea what to do.

"Scout?"

Turning toward the house, he saw Leyna and Brenley standing outside the door. Both wore tense frowns as they stared at him. Scout looked around again. Sand and sun stretched as far as he could see. He shook his head and returned to the house.

"I'm sorry, Brenley. I couldn't...I don't know where Dacey is."

She didn't meet his eyes. "But you remember him and that matters to me."

Leyna watched them without speaking. Scout placed a hand on the archeologist's shoulder and squeezed before walking into the house. Ignoring the women, he studied the house and added his memories of his first trip. He pivoted to face them when his memories provided a clue.

"Brenley, do you remember the other man who was here? The man who gave you the scroll to give to us?"

"Of course." She stood straighter and smiled.

"The drawing of the compass and animals?" Leyna spoke quietly from the other side of the room. "I remember you giving us that and talking to the man."

"Yes," Scout confirmed. He walked closer to Brenley. "Do you know his name or where he lived? He might know where Dacey is."

Brenley's shoulders slumped. "No, I don't. I pay more attention to artifacts than people. I don't know anything about him."

"Maybe we can find something if we search here. There could be a photo or something we can use to find out who he is." Leyna offered the idea while pacing the room.

Scout didn't need to search to know the Snake wasn't there. He did need time to figure out what to say to both women. "Yeah, let's search."

"Do we even know what we're looking for?" Brenley crossed her arms over her chest and stared at the floor.

Approaching her, Scout extended a hand to rest on her shoulder again. Memories of his struggles and doubts made him want to comfort her. She would have more doubts after he shared the truth. When she met his gaze, tears made her eyes bright. He cleared his throat and started talking. "Doc, what would you do at a dig?"

"What?" Both women asked the question at the same time.

Scout clung to the vague plan and plunged ahead. "You study people's lives all the time. Let's study Dacey. You'll help us understand what doesn't make sense. You picked up on the orb being different, right?"

She blinked back the tears and nodded. "The material and colors didn't match the setting. It was an anomaly."

Wincing at her word choice, Scout looked away. Leyna nodded but didn't speak.

"I can do this." Brenley scanned the room then turned back to Scout. "I'm going to grab my tablet so I can take notes."

Leyna moved to his side as the archeologist walked away. "You calmed her down, but I'm still freaking out. Do you really remember a guy I can't remember? Does she?"

Pulling her closer, Scout kissed her until Leyna's arms slid up to his neck. He wanted to distract her, but his thoughts were scattered too. She laughed and patted his chest.

"That's one way to handle stress." Leyna took several breaths and looked around again. "I guess with time travel and magical artifacts as the norm, a few missing memories shouldn't surprise me."

Scout released a half laugh, half sigh. "Yeah, doubting my sanity is kinda my new normal. Welcome to my world."

Scout resisted the impulse to pull the Jaguar or Turtle out of hiding. There was no warmth, no voices to help him find anything in Dacey's home. "Yeah, new normal. It is not easy."

"There's nothing but a name on some auction and museum sites that reference his paintings. I can't believe there's not even a cyber-footprint from this guy." Leyna crammed the tablet back in her bag.

"Actually, we searched for him before and couldn't find anything then either." Scout shrugged when Leyna's mouth fell open then snapped shut.

She paced the room then faced him with hands on her hips. "How exactly am I supposed to know what I've forgotten? How does that even work? I can't believe you remember and I don't."

Moving out of her way when Leyna resumed her pacing, Scout studied the art on the easel closest to him. The familiar image of the cenote taunted him. He trailed a finger along one corner. "Trust me when I say remembering isn't all it's cracked up to be."

"What are you muttering about?" Brenley held her tablet in one hand and tapped the stylus against her leg with the other. She froze next to him with her hand hovering over the painting. "I remember this piece. I showed you the three circles symbol in the rocks."

Her hand fell to her side as the color drained from her face. "How can I remember the art but not the man?"

Scout's hands hovered next to her, but he had no comfort to offer. Relief slumped his shoulders when she turned away and crossed the room. There was only one soft sniffle before she turned back to him. Her face was a blank mask.

"I'm going to start with the back rooms. Leyna, do you mind helping me?"

"Not at all, Doc. Let's go." Leyna blew out a long breath after the archeologist passed her. "Scout, we've gotta figure out what's going on."

After they left, he returned his attention to the paintings. Scout recognized the ones Brenley had previously used to share the three circle formation. He was even able to see it in an unfinished piece of a beach scene. There was no pull toward any sculpture, but he still checked the shelf where the Turtle had been kept. The cold stone of the pieces brought no inspiration. Lost in his thoughts, he found himself standing before the cenote piece once again.

The women's voices as they crossed to another room pulled Scout from his fascinated stare. He turned away from the painting to explore the rooms they had already visited. He tried to keep Dacey in his thoughts while breathing slowly. Panic clawed up from his belly and made both tasks difficult. Pulling up memories of the artist brought both comfort and pain. Scout's memories weren't fading, but that had been his curse since the

Island. He continued to picture Dacey as he walked through his home. Returning to the painting, Scout had no idea how to find the man or explain his disappearance.

"I've cataloged each room, but so far nothing stands out. The pattern of three repeats in his art and his home, but I do not understand the value in that observation." Brenley entered the room and crossed to his side.

Nodding, Scout turned toward the door. "Let's get out of here for now. We can chat at your place."

"Why can I remember the art, the symbolism, but not the man? There's no logical explanation."

Scout tensed when her voice trembled. The archeologist pulled back and cleared her throat.

"I don't think we're going to find anything here, but you still owe me an explanation, Scout."

"We should leave now." Leyna was looking out the windows instead of facing them. "If something bad has happened here, it's not safe for us either."

"It will be safer to explain things somewhere else." Scout picked up the cenote painting and headed to the door.

"Are you going to steal that?" Brow furrowed, Brenley looked at the other paintings. "I feel like I'm forgetting something."

A cold shiver raced down Scout's back. He pivoted but found Leyna standing directly behind him. Her eyes widened as she stared at him from less than a foot away.

"Sorry," Scout mumbled and turned back to Brenley. "Yes, I'm taking it. Once we find Dacey, I'll return it."

The woman sucked in a quick breath before her face cleared. "Okay. He…I don't know what he would want us to do." Brenley's hands balled into fists and the frown returned. She brushed by them to beat a hasty retreat.

Leyna's hand kept Scout in place. "Do you have any idea what's going on? What if I forget other things? How will I know? You still remember everything, don't you?"

"Remembering hasn't exactly been a good thing in the past, but I hope it helps us now." Scout watched the anger drain from Leyna's face. He sighed and stepped away from her. "Like you said, this isn't the place to stay and chat. Let's go."

They found Brenley standing by her vehicle staring at the house. She didn't move even after they opened the car doors and placed their stuff and the painting inside. Leyna shrugged and turned away to allow Scout to speak privately to the archeologist.

"You said there were things we needed to talk about. Can you explain any of this?" Brenley didn't look at Scout to ask the question. Her body remained stiff and unmoving.

"I can't really, Brenley, and I am sorry about that. I didn't want to drag you or anyone into the mess that is my life. I needed answers for myself and that search has put you in danger. I put Dacey in danger." Scout kicked the ground and watched the dust fly. "The FBI agent warned me that I didn't know what I was getting into, that I didn't understand the dangers. He was right."

"It's not your fault." Leyna was facing him again with sympathy shining in her eyes. "You were dragged into this." She stopped there with a glance at Brenley. Biting her lips, she didn't offer further explanations to defend him.

"It is my fault." Scout looked from Leyna to Brenley then back down to the ground. "I've been pushing for answers. Even after the FBI warning, I've kept going. I'm not sure I know how to stop this now."

"We can't go back – we can only move forward." It

was Brenley offering that advice and she nudged Scout with her shoulder. "I study the past knowing I can't change it. I can learn and make different choices now."

Scout ran a hand through his hair and rubbed the back of his neck. "I hope you still feel that way later. I don't really know where to start."

"Scout, you need to—" Leyna tried to warn him again.

"No, Leyna, I'm going to tell her what I know." Scout had no intention of sharing Leyna's past, but he could tell his story. He'd told others who hadn't believed him. "You might want to sit down."

"I'd rather stand." Brenley again crossed her arms and watched him.

"Okay, okay." Scout couldn't seem to find any other words. He flinched when he felt Leyna lean against his back. Her warmth provided more comfort than he'd have liked. "For me, it started in Atlantic City. You said you'd researched the…group hallucination." The words were still bitter on his tongue.

"Yes, hundreds of strangers shared similar stories of a life lived on Atlantic Island. You were one of the survivors." Brenley's tone was matter-of-fact, but she did drop her arms.

"Yeah, survivors." Images of bloody battles and death filled Scout's mind. Some were memories of the Island, but others flashed more brightly as nightmares only found in his mind.

Brenley stepped close enough to place her hand on his shoulder. "Science can't explain it now, but perhaps in the future, you'll get more answers."

"Funny you should mention the future." Scout smirked then blew out a breath. "Remember that orb you knew was different? It really is different. We think it was used to create an alternate reality. Atlantic Island was real, and we lived there for ten years. It wasn't a hallucination, and I'm not crazy. I was a soldier there and people died in horrible battles. They starved and died of injuries. But, I did survive."

Scout wasn't sure if Brenley was more surprised by his outburst or if he was. He'd planned to calmly explain the events to her. He had wanted to offer proof from her experiences to back up the outlandish truth. There was a checklist of things he felt she needed to know to accept that he wasn't crazy. She didn't look convinced when she dropped her hand and stepped back. He took a deep breath and tried once more, but the words still flowed without his permission.

"There were time travelers on Atlantic Island and super soldiers too. Everything was different there, and I don't know if I would have survived much longer." He waved one arm and shrugged. "We were brought back to this reality by Thomas. You've seen the reports – life returned to normal for the Atlantic Island survivors."

"But not for you." Brenley's interruption was surprisingly soft.

"Yeah, not so much for me. Anomaly seems to be my code name. But that's not as important as the orb. See, it's not just the orb that has powers. There are artifacts, Mayan artifacts. The Jaguar you found at your site and the Turtle I found here. Do you still remember Dacey saying the Turtle was mine?" With a harsh laugh, he rolled his eyes. "No, you don't remember and neither does Leyna."

He felt energy roll through his body and pushed away to walk off the rush of power. His muscles bunched and trembled, but there was no one to fight.

There was no room for flight either. Scout turned back and ignored the wide-eyed stares of both women.

"Dacey said the Turtle was mine and called me a Guardian. I'm connected to the artifacts somehow. They are powerful and powerful people want them. Anyone who wants them could be the reason for Dacey's disappearance. The battles on Atlantic Island are over, but there's a war here too. I don't know if we'll survive it. I just know we may have to fight. I had hoped Dacey could share what he knows because I think he knows a lot. What I–"

"Scout!" Leyna pinched his side before stepping around him.

He blinked at her then noticed Brenley had gone completely pale. The archeologist was slumped against her vehicle and sliding toward the ground. Leyna caught her and wrapped an arm around the other woman to keep her upright.

"Let's get back inside."

When Scout stood there staring, Leyna slapped his shoulder.

"Get moving. Back inside. Brenley, you just focus on breathing. We've got you."

8

Scout's hand trembled as he forced the door open and jumped to the side. Leyna kept an arm around the archeologist and half-dragged her in. Brenley's head shook in a series of sharp jerks. She didn't even seem to notice the paintings falling to the floor around her as they stumbled forward.

"Brenley, take a breath, and sit down." Leyna pushed the other woman onto the couch. "He's actually not as crazy as he sounds, but we'll get to that in a minute. Just breathe. Scout, make yourself useful, and get her a glass of water."

Racing to the kitchen, Scout poured the drink from the pitcher. The hibiscus water sloshed over the glass and onto the counter before dripping to the floor. He placed the glass down and wiped up the mess. Balling his hands into fists, he tensed against the tremors rippling through his body.

"Scout, where's the water?" Leyna's words and annoyed tone carried through the house.

He tried to pull himself together as he moved back to

the women. It only took a few steps for him to remember the water and go back for it. Leyna frowned and held a hand out for the glass. Her words were soft when she spoke to Brenley.

"Take a drink of this. We had to wait long enough for Scout to bring it so hopefully, it's good." The joke fell flat. Leyna shrugged and rubbed a hand up and down the archeologist's back. "We will talk about this more. Scout really isn't crazy though I know it seems like he is."

Biting back a laugh at his failed plan, Scout wiped his hands on his pants. "I am so sorry, Brenley."

She glanced up at him and her mouth worked, but no words came out. He wanted to reach for her. Fear of her rejection kept his hands at his sides.

"Take another drink then another deep breath. You've got a little color back in your face and that's good." Leyna stepped in again to help them both.

"The artifacts! Brenley, I have them with me and you can see them. Maybe—"

"She's already seen the Jaguar. Not everyone feels them as you do." Leyna's interruption was softer than earlier. She didn't leave the archeologist's side, but she did reach a hand out to Scout. "You need to take a breath too. We'll talk about this more in a minute."

"I'd like to see the artifacts. I haven't studied the Turtle."

Scout spun away to get both from his bag. He paused to hold them in his hands and the jolt of energy made it easier to breathe. The voices were soft, but the word was clear.

Xibalba
Xibalba
Xibalba

"Scout, are you okay? What does that mean?"

He blinked and realized he had returned to the women and had been speaking the word aloud with the voices in his head. "Xibalba."

Leyna frowned as Brenley nodded. Scout knelt in front of them and held the Turtle out.

"You were the one who translated Xibalba for me, Brenley. Did you wonder where I heard it? You did wonder how we made it here an hour after you called me. You also spoke to the FBI and knew enough to not want their help with Dacey. Dacey! You know your memories have faded, but they aren't gone completely like Leyna's are. My memories of him are clear – I haven't forgotten anything which, makes the anomaly thing good right now." It wasn't the precise list of evidence he'd mentally prepared, but it helped calm Scout to share it. His hands no longer shook when he held the Turtle even closer to the archeologist.

Brenley's hands hovered over the Turtle, but she didn't touch it. "Where did you hear Xibalba?"

Grinning, Scout shook his head. "It's gonna make you think I'm even crazier."

"I do not believe that is possible," Brenley retorted.

"Just remember you said that." Scout met Leyna's eyes before focusing on the archeologist. "I have dreams and have heard voices in my head since the Island. They told me to follow the Jaguar, which led me to you. That's also where I heard Xibalba."

She didn't pass out, but she didn't blink either.

"The people who want the artifacts believe Scout can find all of them. It's one of the few things they agree on." Leyna continued to rub the archeologist's back. Her voice was soft and calm. "I told you – he only sounds crazy."

"If it helps, I'm also under the care of a psychiatrist.

My mom had me tested and everything." Scout forced a short chuckle out to lighten the mood.

"What does your doctor say about the voices?' There was only a slight tremble in Brenley's voice.

Scout regretted sharing that information. "I actually haven't told her. I told Leyna and now you. No one else knows. I have told Dr. Wake about the dreams."

"One of the dreams includes a cenote like Dacey painted." Leyna again tried to redirect the conversation.

"You really expect me to believe in time travel and magical artifacts?" Brenley's expression would have been an exasperated eye roll on anyone else.

Scout couldn't help but laugh. "Can you give me a better explanation for how we got here just about an hour after you called? We'll go back to the exact same time we left, too. I guess we could call you when we get back to prove..." Scout trailed off as his head ached. Time travel discussions always brought a flash of pain.

"No, we can't do that." Leyna glared at both of them. "Time travel is dangerous and must be monitored. There must be rules and order; otherwise we're all at risk."

"At least there are rules for time travel."

Scout exchanged a look with Leyna at the snarky reply from the archeologist. When the girl shrugged, he looked back at Brenley. "I can't tell if you're being sarcastic or not. However, there's a whole organization that monitors time travel. Are you okay talking about this? About time travel?"

"Einstein believed time was a fourth dimension—"

"No, we're not going there," Scout interrupted Brenley. "I don't have all the answers, but I don't think we need to discuss the scientific details floating around in your big brain. Let's keep this simple."

The archeologist waved her hand for him to proceed.

"Atlantic Island was real. The orb you saw is connected and the artifacts too. We don't have all the information. I'm actually not sure anyone else does either. But, we believe the orb is what allowed some people on the Island to have super strength, speed, and healing." Scout paused but neither woman spoke. They also didn't glare, yell, or pass out so he continued. "The Jaguar gives power and the Turtle…the Turtle…."

When his voice trailed off, Leyna cleared her throat. "The Turtle healed Scout. I don't remember Dacey, but I remember the battle here. The two sides that want the artifacts were here." Her voice faltered before she met Scout's gaze again. "There was a fight and Scout was injured. I thought he was going to die."

"You believe the Turtle healed him? Saved his life?" Brenley glanced from Leyna to Scout several times.

"Yes." Leyna didn't look away from Scout to answer the doctor.

"May I touch it?" Brenley gestured to the Turtle.

Scout held it out again and forced himself to pay attention to the archeologist instead of staring at Leyna. "I found it here, and Dacey gave it to me. I was hoping to ask him more questions, but both Hodges' supporters and Thomas' agents were waiting outside."

Brenley studied the Turtle then placed the tip of one finger on a blue spot on the green jade shell.

The Turtle warmed in his hands. Scout's fingers flexed then curled forward as Brenley slid her hand on top of the artifact. Her eyes widened and her mouth fell open. Images of Dacey and his art flashed in Scout's mind – the pictures were bright and detailed. The words were soft, the melody sweet.

The blue jade owl and the patient white snake,
Hunt together during the night,

Prey for prey,
The circles of life rarely ever break,
Destiny is your own to create

The Turtle cooled abruptly, and his mind cleared and quieted. Brenley smiled with wide, watery eyes.

"What happened?" Leyna glanced back and forth before settling on Scout. "Did you see something? Hear the voices?"

Brenley's smile faded and she blinked back the tears, but she didn't remove her hand. "You've had two episodes where I thought you were unwell. Did you see things then?"

"You saw him too?" Scout clutched at her hand, the Turtle trapped between them. "Did you hear it?"

"I saw Dacey and I remembered more of our time. It wasn't everything, and it happened so fast. But, I felt him." Brenley blinked back tears then frowned. "What did you see? Did you hear him?"

Scout pulled back and swallowed the lump in his throat. He stuffed the artifacts away and tried to answer. "I saw his artwork and him. I'm not sure what I heard."

"Is that all?" It was Leyna quizzing him.

Spinning to face her, Scout's frown matched hers. "You think I'm lying about it?" He barked out a laugh, but refused to surrender to her. "My therapist tells me everyone lies so yeah, I guess I am. What about you? What lies have you told, Leyna?"

Brenley again placed a hand on his shoulder. "I still need answers from you, but I think we need a break. I need a break. Let's go back to camp."

9

THE DRIVE BACK TO CHICHEN ITZA WASN'T EXACTLY SILENT. There were long awkward pauses between Brenley's pointed recital of Scout's rambling evidence and her additional information on Xibalba and Mayan mythology. Occasionally, Leyna added a few details from her experiences. Scout kept his mouth shut as it seemed like the archeologist was simply talking to herself to organize her thoughts. While he no longer felt the desire to punch anyone, he wasn't excited to continue a conversation with a careful mixture of truths and lies. He'd lost so many people after the Island; it looked like the good doctor was going to be another one. He closed the door and followed the women to the familiar work tent anyway. It was easier to scan the crowds for danger than to find the necessary words to postpone the inevitable.

"I'm not saying I believe you, but I think we all still need more answers. It seems prudent to continue combining our efforts." Brenley stood at the head of one work table. She tapped a pen against her leg and watched them.

Releasing a pent-up sigh, Scout's head buzzed as a tremor rocked his body. He couldn't resist glancing at Leyna, and she was already turning his way. Her lips turned up in a small smile. Flushed and smiling, he moved to her side.

"You are amendable to continue our working relationship?" Brenley's hands clutched her pen but didn't tap it.

"Yes. I didn't exactly explain things well, but I'm glad you're keeping an open mind. I know we need your help." Slipping an arm around Leyna's waist, Scout pulled her close. "I know I need both of you to help me."

"Then we need to get organized and analyze the situation."

Brenley led their discussion by asking question after question. Leyna offered no details to explain her life, but she did answer some questions about the MMEA and time travel. Scout shared the basics about politics and war on Atlantic Island without revealing much of his personal history. It was easier to share what had happened since his return. He tried to be honest and answer her questions, but it wasn't easy.

"It's kinda hard to find logical answers when you're talking about time travel and super-powered soldiers. I only know what I saw, how I lived on the Island. The time travelers appeared and disappeared at will. Soldiers had extra strength and endurance." Scout tried not to roll his eyes at the ongoing discussion. His relief had been replaced by annoyance.

"And this MMEA is trying to protect our universe?" Brenley ignored him to review her notes and ask the question for the third time.

Leyna stood and nodded, her gaze locked on Scout instead of Brenley. "Yes, Thomas has always tried to preserve life, and he was the one who fought Hodges to save Atlantic Island. He brought the survivors back to us."

The archeologist turned to Scout and pursed her lips. He focused on her and avoided Leyna's frown.

"You don't trust Thomas."

Brenley didn't ask it as a question, but Scout shrugged. "Leyna has known about this longer than me. I'm still trying to figure out what's going on so I prefer not to trust anyone."

"Thomas hasn't contacted you or tried to take away the artifacts. Shouldn't that count for something?" Leyna paced as she twisted the bar earring.

Scout didn't point out that Gerard had also left them alone. "When you're fighting a war on multiple fronts, you have to prioritize. No one seems to know exactly what the artifacts can do. They don't provide an immediate known advantage."

"The Jaguar has given you strength, and the Turtle has healed you." Brenley tapped the pen faster as she flipped through her notes. "I can see your hypothesis connecting the orb, the Mayan artifacts, and the scroll. The solid evidence is limited to personal experience, which leaves it open to interpretation. I cannot determine what the other artifacts could do."

"You have some guesses though, don't you?" Scout jumped on the opportunity to change the subject. "You've studied the Mayans and even worked with Dacey…I'm sorry, I should've stopped while I was ahead."

The archeologist smiled at him and shook her head. "My memories are stronger since I touched you and the Turtle. Don't be sorry about that." The smile faded and the tapping pen grew louder in the silence. "Maybe if we can solve the mystery of the artifacts and find them then Dacey will return."

Scout couldn't force a lie out in response.

"We are agreed that we're focusing on the artifacts then?" Leyna pulled a chair out by Brenley and sat down. "I think we should ask Thomas if they have any new information."

Scout also moved closer to Brenley to study her stoic expression. "Are you sure you're good with all of this? It took me months and several therapy sessions to be as calm as you. Time travel and saving the Universe are pretty big deals."

She chuckled then placed both hands on the table. "I don't have any other answers to explain this. I need the truth, and so do you. The only option is to keep moving forward regardless of any emotional response. And my situation is very different from yours, Scout."

"What do you mean?" If she hadn't appeared sympathetic, he would've pulled back.

"You lived on Atlantic Island. You had people trying to kill you even after you returned." Brenley tapped the pen then placed it back on the table. "I would have doubted my sanity too. I also wouldn't want to trust others. You have placed a great deal of trust in me."

Scout cleared his throat and swallowed around the lump. "You're putting a lot of trust in me too. You already did when you allowed the FBI to cut me loose." A laugh bubbled out as a groan. "Technically, I did steal the Jaguar artifact."

Brenley and even Leyna chuckled at his words. Scout grinned at both of them before giving an exaggerated wink at the archeologist.

"And there's the Southern charm," Leyna mumbled and rolled her eyes.

Standing, Brenley didn't acknowledge their antics. "We should ask this Thomas about the artifacts. The Jaguar was here, but the Turtle was with Dacey. There's no obvious connection so we can't begin to speculate on where the other two artifacts are. We need more information."

"I'll send a message and ask for another meeting." Leyna pulled her phone out and started typing.

"Your dreams and the voices have led you so far." Brenley pulled up a map of the Yucatan peninsula and jotted down a few more notes. She tapped the map and looked at Scout. "Xibalba, the place of fear, is the Mayan Underworld. It's supposed to be an elaborate world with rivers and mountains, even a ball court. The Mayas believed cenotes were entrances. We should visit some and see if…"

When her voice trailed off, Scout laughed. "And see if I hear more voices or get random images in my head? Told you it sounded crazy. We can try whatever location you think might be best. We should also check any places that you connect the Snake to the Mayans."

"There are too many variables. Even El Castillo here in Chichen Itza is linked to Kukulcán or Quetzalcoatl, the feathered serpent. The cenotes and Xibalba are our best clues." The archeologist returned her attention to her tablet.

"What about the color red or East? We still think they are linked to the Snake, right?" Leyna stared at Brenley before continuing. "Are there gods or locations associated with either?"

Brenley didn't even look up from her research. "Muluc is one of the Bacabs, gods of the winds and direction. He represents East, obviously which also links to red."

Leyna opened her mouth, but there wasn't time to speak as Brenley continued.

"Muluc is also the ninth sign of the zodiac. There's a connection to water and sacrifice as well. We could draw a connection to the cenotes."

"Mayan astrology? Like, what's your sign?" Leyna laughed and rolled her eyes.

"That's linked to the stars, right? Constellations?" Scout felt a spark of energy and pictured Orion hunting the Seven Sisters. "Can you align Mayan astrology with other systems?"

When Brenley looked up, it was to frown briefly at Scout. "I haven't studied astrology. I do not know. The Mayan system was math-based and has twenty signs."

The spark of hope became a dull throb in Scout's head. Scrubbing a hand, he stood and stretched. "Okay, I need a break, and we probably need to return home. Brenley, keep researching, and let us know what you find. As soon as we hear from Thomas, we'll update you."

Leyna moved to the tent flap without argument. She shifted her weight from side to side when Brenley grabbed Scout's arm.

"And you'll go back to Virginia and back to the time you left to come here?" She glanced at her watch then frowned at him. "Five hours ago."

"Yeah, don't ask me to explain it. I understand less about time travel than Mayan astrology."

She squeezed his arm before releasing it. "I'm going to keep researching."

"You do that, Doc." Scout paused by Leyna's side and turned back. "Thank you for…well, for everything. You didn't have to…"

Brenley smiled when words failed him. "Scout, I

don't know that I can help you. I do know I'm going to try."

"That's enough for me." Giving the archeologist another big smile, Scout nodded and faced Leyna again. "Lead on, I'm ready for chocolate too."

They didn't speak as they crossed the sandy field to find trees again. The tension returned to itch along Scout's nerves. Rolling his shoulders back, he unclenched his fists and scanned the area. Only Leyna was close enough to hurt him.

"She handled it well. I guess you were right about that." Leyna turned her head toward him but didn't meet his eyes.

"It didn't go exactly as I'd hoped, but Brenley is cool. She wants answers for the sake of answers. She isn't trying to take over the Universe." He lifted his head to the warm sun before digging out a layer of warm clothes from his backpack. It was easier to add the clothes than change completely between time hops.

Leyna's head wasn't through her additional layer when she spoke. "Do you think she's too cool? Most people would have freaked out finding out about time travel for the first time."

Scout waited until her head appeared and held her gaze. "I trust her. I get that you don't and that's okay. I don't trust Thomas. I guess we'll find out later who's right and who is lying."

The simmering anger burst into an inferno. Images of war and death filled his mind as the voices howled incoherently. The coppery scent of blood pervaded his nostrils as he bit back further words.

"Yeah, I guess we will." Leyna stepped close and wrapped her arms around him to take them home.

"You seem tense, Scout." Dr. Wake didn't press him to talk, but she did pause and give him the chance.

Scout could barely make out her reflection in the window. He didn't turn to face her. "The nightmares have returned recently. I'm not sleeping well." It was almost entirely truthful. He hadn't slept much after the FBI interrogation, and he had slept even less since finding out Dacey had disappeared. The nightmares now haunted his waking moments and included seeing his missing friend.

"You are under a lot of stress with your senior year. I doubt you're the only student having nightmares."

His image in the window smirked at her answer. Scout schooled his features and turned to the psychiatrist. "I doubt most seniors are dreaming of war and death." There was no point in sharing that his dreams included jaguars, snakes, and a possible opening to the Underworld. The voices were currently quiet except for the occasional humming of a soft melody.

"I think you might be surprised by others' nightmares. Fear and hope can twist reality into something new and terrifying for each of us." She jotted a few notes down before looking up at him again.

Scout plopped down in one of the visitor chairs and laughed. "Is this you trying to make me feel better? Don't worry – there are other freaks out there too."

Her lips twitched before she shook her head. "Humans are fascinating and most have many layers. How are things with Leyna?"

"Nice segue." Scout kept his body relaxed against the cushions and held her gaze. "I've never asked about her lies. Things aren't as comfortable as they once were."

"And how does that make you feel?"

"Sometimes, I forget you're a psychiatrist then you say something like that," Scout deflected with a laugh. He wasn't surprised when she smiled but stayed quiet. "I feel angry."

Unable to remain still, he hopped up and crossed to the window again. The waves of anger continued whenever he was with Leyna. As they still trained and researched together, it felt like he was drowning under the pressures and—

"Drowning?"

Scout flinched and turned back to her. "What?"

"You were mumbling. I only caught that word. Are those your nightmares or your feelings?" Dr. Wake appeared as calm as ever as she waited for him to continue.

He nodded once and turned back to the window. Taking a deep breath, he tried to find enough of the truth to share to satisfy her. "There's sometimes water in my dreams, but I don't drown. I guess it's just my feelings. The anger…it, um…"

"Feels like a big wave crashing over you?" the therapist prompted softly.

"Yes." He didn't elaborate, but Scout did turn back to meet her eyes.

"We've talked about panic attacks and anger is one variation. Sometimes, we feel fear. Sometimes, we feel tired. As we've discussed, anger is usually the easiest emotion to indulge. It wouldn't hurt to review your coping mechanisms. I know we've encouraged you to focus on the future instead of the past. However, that too puts a lot of pressure on you."

"I don't know what I want to do next." The words held more truth than Scout would have liked.

"Do you need to know right now?"

Scout managed to grin at her. "It would make my life easier if I had some answers."

"I think a lot of people would agree with you on that one too. However, you have something most people don't have." Dr. Wake held his gaze without continuing.

He couldn't hold back a laugh. "I also forget sometimes how different you are from my previous doctors, and that I used to like that about you."

She laughed and nodded. "Okay, I won't make you ask. You have a pivot point in your life that made you question everything. It made you look for options other than the path straight ahead. I know it was traumatic and not what you wanted. It is still a gift to see yourself and the world differently."

"No one has ever referred to last summer as a gift. I don't—" Scout snapped his mouth shut and tried to push back the memories of war and death.

Dr. Wake waited until he looked up. "Gifts don't always come wrapped in pretty paper and ribbons. It is a gift to see in a new way."

Scrubbing a hand over his face, Scout nodded then grinned. "Can I return it or at least exchange it?"

She shook her hand and glanced at her watch before standing. "I have some more information on dream research, and I'm going to ask Natalie to pull the sheets on coping strategies. Those aren't new for you, but it helps to read them periodically. As your life changes, the best strategy for you to handle stress will change as well."

"Thanks, Doctor." Scout accepted the pages she handed him. "You manage to make the craziness seem almost normal."

"Normal is relative." She smiled when he laughed again. "Now, grab a bottle of water and a piece of candy, and let's get you out of here."

It was easier to breathe once he had left therapy, and Scout took several breaths. He promptly coughed when he noticed Gerard standing by his car. A quick glance seemed to prove the teenager was without backup. "I guess my good luck had to run out eventually."

The wide smile again reminded Scout of a wolf in sheep's clothes...or in Gerard's case, a rogue agent hiding as a high school kid. He moved to the driver's side but didn't unlock the doors.

"I'm hurt that you're still so suspicious. Haven't we lived up to our side? No one has tried to take the artifacts from you."

"What would you call the attack in Mexico?" Scout kept his hands loose and scanned the parking garage again.

Gerard tossed back his head to laugh. "That was for Thomas' benefit, not yours. I didn't reveal you and I are friends, did I? I assumed you wouldn't want your girl-friend to know you're lying like she is."

"We aren't friends." Scout pushed the denial out through gritted teeth. He refused to address the comments about Leyna. "Why are you here now?"

"I wanted to see if you got any new information from the archeologist. We haven't located the other artifacts yet, but we've been busy with other things." As he leaned casually against the car, the wide smile almost split the teen's face.

"What other things?" Scout couldn't help but press.

"If we were friends, I'd tell you…" Gerard let the words trail off with a dramatic sigh. "It's nothing you need to worry about right now. So, do you have any guesses on the location of the Owl or the Snake?"

A wave of heat washed over him. It wasn't the anger he'd felt recently, but there was a power, a need. Scout studied the rogue agent then looked around again. "I'm working on it."

"Excellent, glad to hear that. I'm also glad to see you look healthy. That thing in Mexico got a little out of control, didn't it? It looked like you were injured before you slipped away." There was no smile as Gerard's gaze moved to his chest.

Resisting the urge to cross his arms, Scout shrugged. "If you aren't used to war, a little blood can be scary."

Gerard blinked then laughed again. "Yeah, that must be it. Seems like war is coming so I guess I'll get used to it."

Neither looked away and the silence stretched between them. It was Gerard who ended the standoff.

"We might have some information for you. Ask your archeologist about the sundial in the cenote. That might point you in the right direction to find another artifact." Gerard tipped an imaginary hat and grinned. "We'll be in touch."

"Great, looking forward to it." Scout had hoped to anger the teen, but Gerard only laughed again as he walked away.

Scout's phone beeped with a message from Leyna. -*Thomas has info and wants to meet.*

The deafening rush of blood echoed in his ears. He felt the energy flood his body until his fingertips tingled. His phone beeped again.

-*You want to meet him, right?*

He typed a single word in response, agreeing before opening the car and throwing the phone inside. What-ever relaxation he'd gained in therapy disappeared as energy crashed over him. The waves weren't cool like the ocean, but instead hot and heavy. He worked to control his breathing and ignore the painful pressure crushing his heart and lungs. Blinking, Scout stared at his house. He shook his head and breathed out an annoyed sigh. There was no memory in his head of the drive home. Instead, images of blood and storms still filled his mind. He took one step at a time until he crossed the yard to the front door. Maya was sitting quietly waiting for him when he entered the house.

"Hey, girl." He picked the mutt up and closed his eyes. It was quiet enough that he could feel her heart beat against his hand. Flames cooled into a comforting warmth as he continued to cradle the dog against his chest. "You are my best coping mechanism, Maya."

Calmer, Scout returned to the car for his phone. Maya trailed him, barking and dancing. "Yes, we'll work out. Just let me send a quick text. I promise you it's important."

He scanned the messages from Leyna confirming the meeting with Thomas and asking if he was okay. Scout took another breath and smiled at Maya before he sent a text.

-Doc, do you know about a cenote with a sundial?

…HIDDEN IN THE DARKNESS…WAVES OF PAIN WILL DROWN the unworthy… fire from the sky will burn …Xibalba

Scout jerked awake and jumped from the bed. Only wisps of the nightmare remained in his mind tinted by blood and the stench of death. The words echoed in a soft hiss. Maya growled low before moving to his side. Petting her absently, he wiped the sweat from his face with a trembling hand.

"The curse! That's where I've heard the words." Scout picked up Maya and paced the room. Unlike most of his night terrors, the details were hazy. His lingering fear response wasn't. He struggled to slow his breathing as his heart pounded in his chest. There was an ache calling for him to touch the artifacts. He put Maya down and continued to stare at their current hiding place. Fists clenching and unclenching, he pivoted away without reaching for them. His phone beeped a new notification.

Brenley had sent additional notes on the Chichen Itza cenote that did have a sundial. She'd highlighted the name White Road that led northward. Scout moved to his notes to add the information on the Owl's page. He tapped the pen and flipped back to the Snake section, which contained little information.

"If you want me to find the Snake, Dacey, you're gonna have to give me a little help."

Scout didn't expect an answer to the whispered words and didn't get one. He picked up his phone and called Brenley.

"Did you get the information?"

The archeologist rarely wasted time on greetings. However, she was now up at odd hours like him. The search for the artifacts and clues on Dacey was costing them both a lot of sleep. He preferred not to bring it up directly, even though he tried to check on her daily. "Yeah, have you found anything about the Snake?"

"I would have included it if I had."

Scout could hear her typing and the huff of annoyance. "Have you eaten today or yesterday?"

"Have you? You aren't sleeping." The tapping of the keyboard stopped.

He couldn't help but laugh. "I don't think either of us is going to win this argument."

"I wasn't aware that we were arguing."

"Of course not. Okay, let's review what we know then." It wasn't the first time they'd had such calls. It brought surprising comfort for Scout to talk freely about the artifacts. Brenley continued to treat everything with scientific curiosity instead of judgment. Her cool detachment helped keep him calm and focused.

Thirty minutes later, Scout yawned and lay back on the bed. "I don't know how, but we need to focus on the Snake."

"When are you meeting with Thomas?"

"Leyna said he hasn't responded so I don't know. I

guess he has something more important to do." Scout didn't reveal he'd had another secret meeting with the enemy. Brenley had handled the news of time travel well, but he didn't want to push away the one ally he had. Swallowing hard, he clutched the phone tighter. "You told us a translation of the curse…is it…are there other meanings?"

When she didn't immediately reply, Scout sat up and opened his mouth.

"There are always other possible meanings. We still don't have all the information about the Mayas or the artifacts."

Her calm voice didn't bring the comfort it usually did. Scout forced himself to take two deep breaths. "Can you tell it to me again?"

The archeologist was quiet for several seconds. "Scout, curses were often used to scare any would-be grave robbers. Time travel doesn't make them real."

"Time travel shows there's a lot we don't understand." He bit back more words and took another breath. "Please repeat the curse to me."

"The ceiba tree stands strong against the winds of change and isn't broken by the powers hidden in the darkness. Waves of pain will drown the unworthy and fire from the sky will burn any who seek to cut down the tree."

Neither of them spoke for several seconds after Brenley finished. Scout's heart again raced – the words repeating in his head sounded more threatening than her casual recitation. Images of waves and fire brought the hazy feel of the nightmare to life. His breath caught in his throat and heat speared through his stomach. He could see the beach stretched out before him. Bodies, bloody and broken, blocked his path. Waves crashed close enough to cover his shoes as lightning crackled across the sky. A dull thrumming pain settled at the base of his skull.

"I stole the Jaguar from your site." Scout didn't remember deciding to move, but he stood over the backpack with the artifact in his hand. Soft pulses of hot energy rippled from his hand and through his body. The beach scene repeated in his head with crashing waves, death, and fire. When he blinked again, he realized Brenley had been speaking.

"…illogical conclusions based on emotion instead of fact. Any piece could be—"

"How many of those artifacts have time travelers hunting for them? How many could be useful in war?" Scout placed the Jaguar back in its hiding place. A tremor shook his body, but he refused to hold the artifact again. "We don't know yet. We need more information."

It was easier to talk about their search than to share his fears. "You're right, which is hardly surprising." Scout couldn't be sure, but he hoped she rolled her eyes. "How about we visit tomorrow—or today, as it's after midnight?"

"Do you want to see the cenote yourself? I might be able to arrange that."

"It's probably best not to be obvious. Do you have any new theories on the sundial? Anything to connect to the directions or artifacts?"

Her silence surprised him as he'd expected her to rattle off the basic details once again.

"There is another option."

"Well, don't stop there. Another option for what? The sundial?" Scout found himself sitting up in the bed despite Maya's annoyed grumble.

"The curse." Brenley typing was the only sound.

Scout waited as long as he could. "What's the other option?"

"The Mayas weren't like the Incas or Aztecs. They never united into what we would consider a single country. Ruling families held on to their power and kept the country divided." More typing followed when the archeologist again stopped speaking.

"Brenley, you can't leave me hanging." He tried to keep the impatience from his tone, but knew he'd failed when her typing stopping.

"This is why I don't share my theories before I've researched them. It isn't productive to guess."

"But lack of sleep lowers inhibitions like drinking does, and you did share. There's no going back now. Just spit out your sudden inspiration." Leaning back again, Scout smiled to himself.

"Fine." There were a few more seconds of typing before she started again. "In addition to kings and priests, warriors were also in an elevated class. They helped ruling families maintain their power. As you know, human sacrifice was a sacrament. It was the warriors who obtained the sacrifices."

Biting back a sigh, he slouched against the pillow and waited for the woman to get to a point he could understand. It took several more minutes and more references to Mayan gods than he would have liked. Instead of sighing, he started yawning.

"...the curse could have been directed at warriors from other families. The cenote could have been viewed as their personal opening to the Underworld. The unworthy members of another family would have been killed before being allowed in. They would then be an honorable sacrifice to the gods."

"Okay." Scout drew out the word but kept his eyes

closed. Brenley's impromptu lecture acted as a lullaby pulling him toward sleep.

"You aren't a Mayan warrior. Taking the Jaguar wouldn't cause you to be a victim of the curse." There was a triumphant tone in her voice.

He couldn't stop a snort of laughter. "No, I'm not a Mayan warrior, but I see your point. The curse shouldn't be a concern when we have other things to worry about right now."

"Dacey." Brenley's voice softened to a whisper. "I do still remember most things, but I can't help but feel some things were stolen from me. I can't seem to not be bitter about that."

"I am sorry. I wish I'd been able to find him and help you." Scout refused to share the mental ramblings that would either mark him as even crazier or bring her pain. He had no explanation for seeing Dacey in Mexico. "I think we have to keep working on the mystery of the artifacts and hope it brings answers."

The sound of rustling filled the brief silence. "I went back to his house. The paintings are too beautiful to remain there alone so I brought them back with me. If... when he returns, I think he'll want them."

"Yeah, he will." Scout couldn't offer any additional comfort. He could try to distract the archeologist. "Could you send me some information on Mayan warriors? What were they called?"

"Nacom was the head of the unit and elected by the warriors. Holcans were the warriors. I'll send you some information."

"And then maybe get a little sleep or food?" Scout prompted as he settled deeper into his bed. "I'll read the stuff in the morning, but for now, I'm going to sleep and you should too."

1 2

Scout pulled his strike to the left and only grazed Leyna's face. She flinched but continued to fight. His body moved independently of his mind – block the low kick, sidestep the grab, pivot and step away. He could almost feel the energy, angry and heavy, rippling in the air around him.

"You giving up?" She panted the question with a laugh. "It's not even spring, but I'm drenched in sweat. I'll get our water."

The words were a distant buzz in Scout's head as he stared at her flushed face. She grabbed a towel and poured a little water on it before wiping her face. Blood still roared through his veins – hot and pulsing. Familiar images from his nightmares flashed brightly and painted the quiet forest in a red haze.

Xibalba

Waves of pain

Follow the Jaguar

Xibalba

The water bottle smacked his chest before landing on

the ground with a thud. The voices quieted and the bloodstains faded into nothing. He looked around and found Leyna staring at him with her mouth hanging slightly open. She snapped it shut and walked to him – her movements were exaggerated and slow.

"Scout? Are you back with me? Are you okay?"

"Yeah, I'm fine." He picked up the bottle and took a long drink with his eyes closed. Leyna had continued her approach and stood mere inches from him. Scout twisted his frown into a smirk. "If you wanted to be closer, you only had to say something."

Her mouth opened, he took advantage and tugged her forward into a kiss. She stiffened then stood on her tiptoes to deepen the kiss. He softened his grip and let himself be distracted too. The new heat in his blood had nothing to do with the artifacts. They were both breathing hard when they pulled back.

"Keep training…or get a little cardio in?" Scout grinned before pressing kisses along her cheek and throat.

"As tempting as that is, I think we need to talk." Leyna broke away and put several feet between them. She got another bottle of water while avoiding his gaze.

Nodding even though Leyna couldn't see him, Scout picked up the bottle he didn't remember dropping. His body cooled fast and resulted in a shiver running down his spine.

"Are you sure you're okay?" Leyna's shoulders hunched as she wrapped her arms around her body. "Things have been weird lately. I know there's a lot going on, but I thought you might want to tell me what you're thinking."

He'd known she would push eventually – she wasn't that patient, and he wasn't as good at hiding things as she was. The anger he'd tried to ignore flared in his chest. Leyna again closed the distance between them and placed her hand over his heart.

"We're partners, right? You can talk to me."

Scout placed his hand over hers and smiled. "We are partners, and I know I can talk to you. There is a lot going on, and the nightmares have become a constant thing so I'm not sleeping much." He cut off the ramble of words and squeezed her hand before dropping it.

"The same cenote dream?"

"Yes." Scout lied without flinching.

"And Brenley has no new information on any cenotes which connects to the artifacts?" Leyna dropped her gaze and tugged on her earring.

"You know the good doctor. She isn't much on sharing ideas without evidence. She's sent a couple of links about archeological digs, but I'm waiting until she gives us a bottom line." It was easier to share the truth even if it was only a partial one. It was even easier to try another distraction. "Any word from Thomas or Marcus? I thought Thomas wanted to meet."

"I'm sure Hodges' supporters are causing problems." Leyna met his gaze but didn't elaborate further.

"Why don't we do a couple more katas then go for a jog? I have some homework to finish and need to walk Maya." Scout didn't want to have another argument about trusting the MMEA.

Leyna smiled and nodded. "You should've brought her with you. It's been a while since I've seen the pup."

"Next time." Scout began a familiar kata at a slow pace. There were no more images or voices as they completed their training.

He jogged the trail behind Leyna until they reached

the park. The cold weather meant there was no one to disturb them as they slowed to a walk then stretched.

"If we can get Brenley to share her ideas, I can help research. Should I send her a message?" Leyna stepped a leg back into a lunge and stared forward.

"I'll call her tonight and get a list." Scout didn't add how frequently he spoke to the archeologist.

Nodding, Leyna said nothing else, even after they got in his car and he drove to their usual café. He was placing their order when she grabbed his arm.

"Get it to go. You have homework and so do I."

"Sure, good idea."

They shared a barely-there kiss before she headed to the left and he returned to his car. Scout refused to turn and watch her. Getting into the car, he glanced at the rearview mirror as she turned the corner and disappeared from view. A sudden ache pounded through his skull with enough force to have him seeing stars. He pressed both hands against his forehead and tried to breathe through the pain.

New images flashed behind his eyes. An orange and pink sunrise peeking over trees – a flash of dark brown eyes – cool water under a blanket of bright stars – sharp spices warmed his tongue.

Find the Snake, Scout.

Jerking his head up, Scout opened his eyes and stared at a hazy image of Dacey. The artist stood in front of Scout's car. Behind him wasn't a small-town street, but a forest with a single large stone snake.

"Dacey?" Scout spoke aloud.

Xibalba.

Dacey's mouth didn't move; the single word echoed in Scout's head. As he watched, the Mexican forest receded into a familiar small-town America scene. The greys of the street and buildings were familiar but not comforting. Brenley's ringtone had him grabbing blindly for his phone.

"Brenley."

She waited for a single second before launching into an update. "Ek Balam is north of Chichen Itza. As it's related to the Jaguar and Owl, I think we should visit it. There are ruins there too. Dzibilchaltún has the Temple of Seven Dolls and more Spanish influence. It is also north so it shouldn't be overlooked. I told you of Ek Balam previously. Did you visit it then?"

Still staring at the empty street, Scout cleared his throat. "No, we didn't. Wait, north?"

"Yes. The road from the cenote is the White Road. Didn't you read the research I sent you?" Brenley sounded very much like a disappointed teacher chastising a lazy student. "You are the connection, but I am trying—"

"I know," Scout interrupted without looking away from the street. "I think we should focus on the Snake, not the Owl."

"We've found no evidence linking to the Snake."

"Xibalba." Scout could almost feel the voices humming in his head. "We know the Snake relates to red and east. We know Chichen Itza has snakes."

Her silence made him grit his teeth. "We might not always be able to proceed logically, Brenley. Have you been paying attention to the craziness of our world?"

Scout closed his eyes and let his head flop back against the headrest. A flash of pain behind his eyes disappeared quickly. His guilt remained and grew as Brenley stayed quiet. "I'm sorry. You've been a friend and your knowledge and research saved my sanity. I shouldn't take a bad mood out on you."

"Is that all it is?"

Her tone was softer and allowed Scout to breathe. He choked on the breath when she continued.

"We've established that you aren't normal. Is a bad mood all you're experiencing?"

"You know I have an actual therapist, right?" Scout forced himself to grin and even chuckle at her bluntness. "Not to mention, lack of sleep makes me cranky. I'm sure that's something you can relate to, Doc."

"Lack of sleep does have effects similar to drinking."

"Apparently, I'll be a moody drunk once I'm legal to drink." Scout tried to keep the conversation light. "I'm heading home now. Don't forget to eat and get some sleep yourself."

"You too." She clicked the phone off without further words.

Scout shook his head and started his car. Sleep called to him, but so did the need for answers.

13

STILL SLEEP-DEPRIVED, SCOUT STUMBLED TO THE KITCHEN later than normal. His mom smiled and ruffled his hair.

"I thought you were out walking Maya. You don't normally sleep this long." His mom was already dressed and the kitchen showed no signs of a morning meal.

"Where's Dad?" Scout rubbed his eyes before giving Maya's ears a scratch.

"His meeting last night continued this morning and he has tennis after that. We're going to a charity auction tonight." She handed him a cup and smiled. "Tea is better, but there's research in favor of black coffee too."

He gulped down half the cup before realizing his mom had also sat down at the table. Running a hand through his short hair, Scout did a quick mental review of the weeks since the FBI interview. His current issues were things he'd hoped to keep from his parents. They had backed off the constant vigilance—his grades were good, pre-spring tennis was going well, and he'd submitted all his college applications on time.

"The event tonight is at the museum. They are raising

money to bring more kid-friendly exhibits for the summer." She smiled at him before smoothing out non-existent wrinkles from her blouse.

He wasn't fooled by his mom. His dad was known as a clever businessman, but Scout had never seen him win an argument against his mom. She was the one who always told him "You catch more flies with honey than vinegar." She wouldn't say such things in public though. Grinning, Scout leaned back in his chair and waited.

"Part of the money raised will be allotted to interns. They have a position on the marketing team which your dad and I think will be a wonderful opportunity for you to make business contacts. Now, it won't be something that impacts your college applications as you should start getting those acceptances next month. It is still an interesting opportunity, don't you think?" She held his gaze with a hopeful smile.

"The museum? That's not really how I'd planned..." Scout shook his head and stopped speaking. Nothing in his life was as he'd planned.

"Dr. Wake noted that your homework included a lot of history papers, even for your psychology class. She also pointed out that your grades on those assignments were always high. We weren't aware of your interest in history before. The museum needed interns last summer too." She faltered and looked away.

Scout reached across the table to take her hand. "It's a new interest, Mom. Even you couldn't have dragged me there kicking and screaming last year." He didn't need to mention that the Atlantic City trip had been entirely his idea. It'd be easier to blame his parents, to blame anyone really, but that choice had been his. He wasn't surprised by the push of those memories—crashing waves, trembling sand, sun and storms.

"Scout?" His mom squeezed his hand. "We always want to support your choices, but we are your parents. We want to protect you too."

"I know. I've always known, even when I didn't listen to you." He grinned and winked at her. "I love you too, Mom."

She shook her head and pulled her hand back, but she also returned his smile. "Good. I guess that means you'll apply for the internship then. Mr. Pendergast is the gentleman you need to speak to and he's expecting your call."

Before he could reply, she slid a business card across the table. "Make sure you dress appropriately for the interview, and no, Maya shouldn't go with you."

"I'll call him today." Scout knew he'd been played, but he couldn't help but laugh.

"Good boy." She brushed a kiss against his temple and ran her fingers through his hair again. Placing her hand on his shoulder, she waited for him to look at her. "We love you, Scout."

He felt his face flush at the words. His family had always spoken more of duty than love before the Island. Scout wasn't sure if they had changed or if he simply saw them differently. It was almost—

"Scout, don't forget to clean your room today. I'll take the dry-cleaning in on Monday, but you have to do your laundry." The front door closed after those loving words from his mom.

Laughing, Scout finished his coffee and chatted with Maya about plans for their day. They moved to the back yard to train after he'd had a protein bar and she'd finished her kibble. He looked around the familiar setting as the dog sniffed her usual path to take care of her business.

Hidden in the darkness...waves of pain will drown the unworthy...fire from the sky will burn...

Bits of the curse played on repeat in his head. A buzzing pain accompanied the voice; Scout squeezed his eyes shut and winced. When he opened his eyes, the back yard shimmered and blurred into a haze of pinks and oranges. He looked away again and tried to take a steadying breath. The colors faded to reveal a Mayan pyramid. A shadowy snake slithered down the steps to meet the snake sculpture positioned at the bottom. The stone animal rumbled before its eyes glowed red.

Hidden in the darkness...waves of pain will drown the unworthy...fire from the sky will burn...

The words faded along with the pyramid until Scout was again staring at his back yard. Maya bumped against his legs and released a series of sharp barks.

"I think we need to step up our training." He had to pause to breathe. There was no longer pain nor hallucinations, but fear made his heart race. When Maya stood on her back legs to scratch at his thighs, he picked her up and cuddled her close.

"Yeah, okay. We're gonna train now, girl." Scout held her another few seconds then placed her on the ground. A quick glance showed there was no change in his surroundings. "Darkness, pain, and fire. Okay. How exactly do we train for that?"

Maya's bark provided no answer, but she did make him smile. "I guess we have to try something new and different, right? We do have the place to ourselves and can hide all evidence if it goes wrong."

He ignored the immediate thought of his family home burning down. Swallowing hard, he studied the layout of obstacles once more. "Maya, let's get you inside."

The dog trailed obediently, but whined when he closed the door. Scout quickly rearranged the course order and positions. He also added new obstacles and even hid some of the treats he kept in his pocket. Going back inside, he picked Maya up and kept her turned away.

"No peeking, pup. You're going to run the full course in order." He placed her on the ground and gave the hand signal.

Pivoting, Maya headed to the left but skidded to a stop. Her head tilted to the side then she plowed ahead. One pile of treats distracted her for a few seconds, but his whistle had her sprinting forward once again. She completed the course in the new order twice. A brown blur leapt into his arms minutes later.

"Good girl, yes, you are a good girl." Scout twisted his head to avoid her tongue connecting with his open mouth as he continued to praise her.

He went through his usual routine in reverse order. Lunges, bear crawls, push-ups, pull-ups, and sprints were simple and familiar moves. Before his second round, he practiced a series of strikes and blocks he and Leyna used to train. He was winded by the third round of exercises.

"Let's go, Maya!" It was his turn to follow the pup through the new course.

"Stay." Even as he gave the command, Scout worked through two more rounds of the basic moves. He then turned back to the course to crawl through tubes, run over a short balance beam, jump over empty boxes, and dive through the hoop. On the other side of the yard, he completed a final round of the basics.

"Maya, now!"

The dog ran over him as he crawled through the last

tunnel. She was doing her usual victory dance when she returned to the door. Collapsing on the ground, Scout laughed and waited for her to return to him. Maya bathed his sweaty face in puppy kisses until he pulled her into his arms and stood.

"That's enough for now, but we're going to have to invite Leyna to join…unless you think you can rearrange the course for me." The dog twisted to try and lick his face again. "Yeah, you're too sweet for warfare training, aren't you?"

The joke fell flat when he realized Leyna wasn't too sweet. She also wasn't as sweet as he'd first thought. He pushed the first shared memories aside. It was easier to think of her as Thomas' agent and his personal time travel guide. He'd kept a distance even with his mom asking the occasional question about her.

"I'm not inviting her home with us." He grumbled to himself and put Maya down again. Dragging the training course back to storage helped ease some of his frustration. Thinking of an alternative location brought a smile.

After a quick shower and internet search, he led Maya out the door and into his car. He packed extra water and snacks for all three of them and headed toward another city park. The cooler weather again worked in his favor as the playground was empty.

He fired off a quick message to Leyna with the address – *New training option today. Join me and Maya?* She responded immediately and Scout proceeded with the plan. He was waiting in the park and watched his partner approach with a smile.

Leyna kissed his cheek before she knelt to pet Maya. He cleared his throat and waved a hand to the playground.

"Are we Traveling back to your childhood?" Her brow furrowed as she stood with a final pat on the dog's head.

"Haven't you seen the latest exercise trends? Basically, it's about getting outside and moving, but we're going to make the game more fun." Scout continued to grin and even winked at her.

"You can't be serious." She gave the setup another look before shaking her head. "How hard can it be if rugrats play here?"

14

"I SAY WE LET THE RUGRATS KEEP THEIR PLAYGROUND." Leyna was stretched out on the cold ground with an arm slung over her face. Her skin was flushed and glowing; her lips quirked into a smile.

"Feeling your age, witch?"

"Watch it, soldier boy. I kicked your ass when I picked the order. And, I totally smoked you on the rope wall." Leyna giggled and rolled on her side to face him.

Scout's grunt wasn't quite a laugh. He swiped a hand to remove the spilled water from his chin. "I have bigger feet. That's the only reason I got stuck and you didn't."

"Whatever you need to tell yourself to make ya feel better." She pulled her legs closer to her chest and chuckled.

"What about the monkey bars? That was all me." He flexed his arms and winked.

She swatted half-heartedly at his leg. Grumbling, she rolled over onto her back again. "It was fun, but I am so tired. I know we should stretch." Leyna made no effort to move.

93

Scout rolled his eyes and refilled Maya's water dish. After grabbing snacks and another water, he plopped down next to Leyna. She didn't even open her eyes when she smacked his thigh and smiled. His muscles were trembling, but there was a giddiness inside that made him want to laugh. It had been fun to climb, run, and spar as part of their training. Maybe it was the brightly colored obstacles or silly pictures posted throughout. Whatever it was, he felt good. He hadn't felt this peculiar exhilaration in a while; he hadn't felt it since before the Island. Laughter dying on his lips, he held the extra bottle of water out for Leyna and ignored the memories. Maya curled up between them. "Here, you need to rehydrate. You should probably put your jacket back on too."

Groaning, she reached for the water and tried to pour it in her mouth without lifting her head. She choked and sputtered as she sat up. "You really are trying to kill me, aren't you?"

"At least you aren't the one bleeding." Scout lifted the bandages to check the road rash on his palm and forearm. He'd misjudged the jump over the sandbox and had landed in the parking lot instead of the grass. It was hardly the worst injury he'd received.

"I told you not to try that jump. Let me see." She scooted closer and wrapped a hand around his arm. "Do you think you'll heal faster since you have the Turtle?"

"Like some kind of immortal god or vampire? I could go for that." Scout grinned then pulled his arm back once she'd pinched him. "I don't have the Turtle with me so I doubt I'll heal."

Leyna stuck her tongue out and sighed. "I've been wondering if having them around you and using them has some lasting effect. We really don't know much about them."

"Thomas tested the Jaguar but didn't tell me anything about the results." Scout looked down at Maya as he rubbed her belly, but he also watched Leyna from the corner of his eye. She plucked at the brown grass. He tried to ignore the anger to get answers. "Has he responded about another meeting? We could ask him then what they've found out."

"I haven't heard anything else from him. We should definitely ask when we meet him. What if the artifacts aren't good things? I mean, if the rebels think they can be used to beat Thomas, that can't be good."

Scout shrugged despite the tension in his shoulders. "I don't really want to get between them, but I don't think the artifacts are evil. They have only helped me. I do think even good things can be used in evil ways."

She seemed poised to argue but then nodded. "The Turtle saved your life. I know that and I'm glad."

"But you are still worried." The tension eased once again when she blushed and looked away. He felt too good to question the return of the warmth or happiness filling him. Scout leaned forward to kiss Leyna's cheek. "We'll ask Thomas. For better or worse, I'm connected to the artifacts. That seems to be the only thing everyone agrees on."

"That connection doesn't mean you have to risk yourself." She shook her head with a frown. Her hair brushed against his mouth. "I know they're important and it's your job or whatever to find them. I get that. I just..."

"You just what?" Scout prompted after several seconds of silence.

Leyna twisted her earring and glanced around the park. "I guess I just had different expectations. This isn't how I thought it'd go."

"You thought it'd all be margaritas on a Mexican

beach?" Pleasant memories of that night warmed his heart and body. He pressed more kisses along her face and nuzzled her hair away from her ear. "That was a spectacular night."

"Yes, it was, but I didn't expect that either." Leyna lowered her head and continued in a soft voice. "I always pictured what it would be like living outside the Fair. I thought the world had changed from fear and hate. That it had evolved into something more."

She lunged to her feet and dusted off her pants. "Sorry to ramble. Are we finished for the day?"

Scout stood slowly. Her words repeated in his mind, creating a heady buzz that did nothing to dispel the warmth. "Marcus rescued you from Salem and that terrifying existence."

"Yes." Leyna flicked a frown his way before looking around again. "What does that have to do with anything?"

"You found something good for yourself even then." He stepped close enough to cup her face and make her meet his gaze. "You wanted something good for yourself in this time too, didn't you?"

She blinked rapidly but didn't look away. "I wanted to find something normal."

"I understand wanting to be normal." Keeping her close, he pressed a line of kisses from her temple to the edge of her mouth. "I think that's one of the many things we have in common."

Leyna tilted her head so they could kiss. When he brought her flush against his body, the gentle warmth exploded into sizzling heat. It spread through his body then pooled low in his stomach. His hands moved over every bit of skin he could reach. The rasp of her short nails against his arms left a trail of goosebumps in their wake. Leyna's unique scent filled his nostrils and brought more images of the Mexican beach. Sunset pinks, ocean blues, and margarita greens colored his memories of their first date. The need for oxygen made them separate mere inches.

"Neither of us is normal, but I couldn't stay away from you."

The words sent an icy shaft through Scout's heart. He eased back further but forced his mouth into a smile. "No, you couldn't."

She laughed and laid a hand on his chest. "We wouldn't have become partners if I had stayed away. Where would you be without me?"

Before she could close the distance to kiss him, Scout tapped one hand against his leg and gestured. Maya barked and circled them.

"What the...Maya? Is she okay?" Leyna crouched low, but the dog continued to circle and bark.

Scout took a deep breath and stilled his hand. Maya stopped and sat by his feet. "Definitely weird, but she looks okay. I think we are done for the day, but we'll come back again."

"Oh, okay. It was harder than I thought it'd be. But I can understand training to learn to adjust to new things too. It wasn't something I've ever thought about, but I guess war is very different than training." She bounced lightly on the balls of her feet.

"No plan of action survives the first battle." Scout remembered being told that. He also remembered learning the truth of it. A numbing cold spread from his chest to chill his body.

15

Scout left a note to assure his mom he had called about the museum internship, then he avoided his parents. Separating from Leyna hadn't brought a clear head, but anger had chased the chill away. He did the bare minimum to prepare for sleep and flopped down on his bed twenty minutes later. Maya was already there waiting for him.

"You were a very good girl today. If you hadn't barked to interrupt us...that deaf dog training really does rock, doesn't it?" He refused to feel guilty about using a smart battle strategy. Leyna was Thomas' agent and had an agenda.

No longer ready to sleep, he paced the room before grabbing his phone. Brenley had sent more notes for his review. He'd also sent her a short message reminding her to eat and sleep. Her notes were as organized as ever and were now separated by Owl and Snake. There was little new information for either, unfortunately.

"It's not new to us, but that doesn't mean it can't

serve a purpose." Scout laughed and rubbed Maya's belly. "There's nothing wrong with having a strategy."

He picked Ek Balam and the White Road to start Leyna's research efforts. If she shared the information with Thomas, it would send them after the Owl instead of the Snake. "Now, we need Brenley to actually find something on the Snake."

Maya snored as he tapped his phone and considered his options. He pitched his voice low to review the information. "The voices said Xibalba, and Dacey said to use the artifacts to find the Snake. Red – east – dawn – fire."

He froze as he remembered the curse. "Fire from the sky."

A quick search of Brenley's recommended sites brought up information quickly. He bookmarked all the mythology, historical, and archeological websites she'd shared. The research papers were also saved, even though he hadn't read them all.

"Okay, Itzamna. Let's see what it means to be the ruler of the heavens." Scanning the article added new notes, which he wasn't ready to share with anyone. "Fire, writing, calendars, knowledge. Okay then, you're on the list."

"Who else is connected to the sky?" He continued to search and scroll through various gods and goddesses before stopping on an image of a snake.

"Huracan – God of Storms and Chaos whose leg is drawn as a snake. That sounds promising." He added more notes and even sent Brenley a message asking about both deities. Stretching with a yawn, he rubbed his eyes and blinked to clear his vision. There wasn't an immediate reply from Brenley. "Huh, maybe she's resting finally."

Maya snuffled in her sleep but otherwise ignored

him. Scout put aside the tablet and squirmed into a more comfortable position on his half of the bed. Closing his eyes, he counted his breaths and tried to relax. Memories of sunset on a Mexican beach slid into his mind as he drifted into sleep. Beautiful sky, spicy scents, and Leyna's warmth pressed into his body.

Memories of a magical night were replaced by nightmares.

Scout expected the cenote; the ocean waves crashing over him were a surprise. He pulled himself out of the water then slid and stumbled across the beach. His skin tingled and his muscles trembled against the chill of the water. Salt coated his tongue and stung his eyes. A series of pops and hisses demanded his attention. He fell forward when he twisted to look around. Flipping onto his back, he rolled away before the fireball landed on him. Bright orange comets hurled toward him as fire fell from the sky. Sparks burned his skin while he scrambled back to his feet. Choking on acrid smoke, his lungs burned when he ran. An endless beach stretched in front of him; an angry ocean nipped at his heels.

Xibalba…follow the Jaguar…Xibalba

A heavenly chorus chanted the words in time with his pounding feet. Fear spiked more painfully than the stinging fire and icy water. Face-planting in the sand, he pushed up, then froze and stared at the paw print.

"Jaguar." He breathed the word and time stood still. The world before him darkened to pitch black.

Xibalba…follow the Jaguar…Xibalba

Scout jerked forward at the howl of words. He blinked and stared at his bedroom. Maya lay curled by his hip, warm and comforting. Sighing, he turned to lie on his back. The man sitting on the foot of his bed smiled at him.

"Dacey? What are you...okay, I'm still dreaming." Sitting up, Scout shook his head then laughed. "At least this is better than drowning and burning."

"I feel like you are damning me with faint praise. You should be glad to see me."

"Damning you? Okay, whatever. I would be glad to see this dream you if it was my subconscious sharing some insight into Brenley's research. If you are here to mock, I think I'd rather go back to the fireballs." Scout stood and looked down at his body. There were no marks from the beach, a sniff confirmed his shirt didn't smell smoky. "You've gotta love dream cleaning."

"And if I told you this wasn't a dream?"

"You look like a ghost. I can almost see through you. Are you really going with this is real?" Grabbing his water bottle, Scout downed half of it before looking at the artist again. "I'd love to see you in the real world. Brenley would love—"

"She's too smart for her own good. You shouldn't be using her." The playful tone was replaced by a grumble when Dacey interrupted him. Even ghostly in appearance, his nostrils flared when he stepped in front of Scout and glared. "It is your job to find and protect the artifacts, not hers."

Guilt and anger warred inside Scout; anger easily won. He lifted a hand then balled it into a fist. "This job didn't exactly come with instructions. And it wasn't one I wanted either. If you really want to help, cut the crap and give me straight answers."

"Xibalba—"

"That's what I mean! The mystical clues aren't working for me, and not even Brenley is smart enough to figure them out." Scout smirked when the other man spun away. The guttural word wasn't even English, but it was easy to see Dacey was annoyed. "I can't believe my dream version of you is more of a pain in the ass than the real one."

Dacey turned to frown then rumbled out a half-laugh. "It doesn't bother you that you dreamed about me? I am a good-looking guy, I guess. A lot of people fall for artists, but I hadn't realized you—"

"Get over yourself." Scout rolled his eyes. "Seriously though, do you have anything helpful to add?"

"How hard is it to find your place of fear?" The smug expression became a frown again. "Can you feel the shifting sands? Things are changing – new players joining an old game. The Owl and the Snake are being hunted. It is the Snake you need to find first."

Scout leaned against his desk and crossed his arms over his chest. "I guess this nightmare isn't going to end until my brain reveals…okay, yes. I know the players already. There's Thomas leading the MMEA and some guy Hodges has supporters like Gerard. They think the artifacts can be weapons."

"Of course they can. What use would warriors have for them otherwise?"

Ignoring the interruption, Scout sighed. "Gerard says they're okay with me finding them, but I trust him even less than I trust Thomas. I think it's easier for both sides if they let me find them and take them from me."

Dacey remained silent but stared at him.

"It's a smart strategy. If you have multiple fronts to defend or advance, you put your efforts where you need to first. Leyna can't feel anything from the artifacts, so I guess most others can't either. We've already found two. Why not let me do the work then take them?"

"You must protect the power. That is your job as Guardian."

"Again, not a job I ever wanted or accepted." Scout spat out the words and looked away. "I don't even know what it means to be a Guardian."

"It means that power corrupts. A Guardian can balance the energies and protect the world with a warrior's honor."

Shaking his head, Scout stared at the artist once more. "I think you need to find another Guardian if it's a warrior you need. I did the soldier thing on the Island and never want to do that again. Even if I can find them, I don't think I can stop Thomas or Gerard. I know I can't stop both of them."

"There is no other Guardian." Dacey crowded into his space and glared down at him. "You are the Guardian now."

Scout latched on to one word only. "Now? Wait, was there another Guardian before me?"

Backing away, the artist again snarled more gibberish Scout couldn't understand.

Dacey lifted his head to stare at the ceiling. "There was another Guardian. He failed and many innocent lives ended in blood. You don't have that option."

16

Scout reached for Dacey when the man's image shimmered. The artist disappeared into thin air. The sharp beep of Scout's alarm drew him back to reality. Maya barked and leapt off the bed to paw at his legs. He stood next to the desk as he had in the dream.

"Not the worst dream, girl, but not the best either. Just wait a second, Maya." Scout sat at his desk and jotted down as much as he could remember about the conversation with Dacey. Without thought, he reached for his phone to call Brenley.

"Have you already read my e-mail?" The archeologist's voice came through loud and clear despite the earlier hour at her location.

"No, that's not what this is about. Can I tell you about my dream?" He rubbed his neck and winced at the pain.

After a longer than normal pause, Brenley cleared her throat. "I thought you said you had a therapist."

He couldn't help laughing. "Yeah, I do. One interpretation of dreaming is that our subconscious is working through problems."

"And your subconscious provided answers we need last night?" Skepticism was obvious in her tone. "It's not what I would consider research. However, you have previously pointed out the strange qualities of our unique situation. Tell me about your dream."

"The first part was obviously the curse. I was on a beach and waves were trying to drown me while the sky spit fireballs down." He rolled his shoulders and neck, but the ache lingered. "And no, we don't need to psycho-analyze that one. It's the next part I think is important." Stopping, Scout remembered her emotional response to losing Dacey. There had been no more breaks in the doctor's tough, logical façade, and he didn't want to be the one to bring her pain.

"Scout? What's the next part?" The tap of her pen against a hard surface echoed after her words ended.

"I saw Dacey." Scout held his breath and waited.

"Dacey." The tapping stopped, but her fast breaths filled the silence. "It makes sense that we'd dream about him. We can't explain what has happened, what is happening. The chemistry of a human brain—"

"He talked to me about the artifacts." Scout wanted to ask what she had dreamed about, but he needed to focus on the new points from his own subconscious. "He talked about finding Xibalba and guarding the artifacts."

"Is that all he said?"

Scout flinched at the tremor in her voice. "My dream version of him was a smartass."

Brenley released a watery laugh. "The real version is a smartass too. He doesn't like people any more than I do."

"He doesn't seem to like me. He basically complained

that I wasn't doing my job. There was something about weapons and balancing power. The Guardian needs to balance the power, I think.

"And you're the Guardian." Brenley started tapping the pen again and her voice returned to its normal tone. "It makes sense that the dream Dacey is focused on the Snake because you are. Did he say anything else?"

Scout glanced at his notes and tapped his pen in time with hers. "He mentioned that the last Guardian had failed."

The silence was longer this time. He stopped tapping and cleared his throat. "I think that's my personal fear coming through."

"Not necessarily," Brenley disagreed. "The scroll shows all four together. We are assuming the Atlantic Island orb was used to inspire their creation. It would make sense that all four directions would be created at the same time. That much power would need to be protected. It wouldn't be the first time a warrior held a place of authority and prestige for the Mayas."

"I'm trying to follow your thought process, Doc. I think I need a buy a vowel."

"Buy a vowel? How would that help?"

Scout laughed at her response and could imagine her frown. "For a brilliant archeologist, you do miss some things. Let's focus on the idea of a previous Guardian. Keep explaining it to me please."

"We didn't find all the artifacts together in a place of honor, Scout. If the Guardian had protected them, that's how we should have unearthed them. Instead, we've only found a few scraps of information hidden from most scholars. There are many mysteries about the Mayas, but this is the first time I've heard of animal sculptures representing power and granting special abilities to a select few."

"Which would mean the Guardian failed. The pieces were somehow lost over the centuries as well as any reference to the orb or even powers." Nodding to himself, Scout grinned then laughed. "You are absolutely right again, Doc. Thank you."

She brushed his appreciation aside. "It's a logical conclusion. That Guardian failed, but someone somewhere knew about the pieces. They knew enough to start looking for them and to connect them to you."

"I think you missed one key 'some', Brenley." Scout smiled at the annoyed huff from the archeologist. "Someone somewhere…at some *time*. There are time travelers out there, and we have to think they know more than us."

"If they knew more, they wouldn't need you to find the artifacts."

"Good point." Scout put the phone down and hit speaker so he could scroll through his notes again. "We do need to find them. I'm going to send my notes to you from the dream. I will review whatever you've sent too, but I also have homework to finish for tomorrow and a family lunch."

He added a few points to clarify his rambling as the memories of ice and heat on the beach sent a chill down his spine. Omitting his feelings, he added details that could help. "Brenley? Sorry, I was updating my notes and got lost in it. You still there? You okay?"

"How do you do it?"

Peering at the phone, Scout tried to follow the jump in her thought process. She continued before he could put the pieces together or ask a question.

"You speak of family dinners and homework in the

same breath as time travel and alternate universes. How do you do that?"

"I could send you the coping mechanisms from my therapist who, by the way, has told me that everyone lies." Scout chuckled then sighed at the silence on the other end of the phone. "I'm sorry. It's easier to deflect."

"Yes, it is. Do you lie?"

His lips twitched at her monotone agreement and blunt question. "Everyone lies. I think the trick is not to lie to yourself. I wasn't kidding when I told you I thought I was crazy. There were days like that on the Island, and there are still days like that here. I keep waiting to wake up and find out it's been a nightmare. It's hard to trust I see the truth in the world."

Her ongoing silence encouraged him to continue.

"You said we have to keep moving forward. That's a soldier's mantra. It's not safe or smart to sit and wait for things to change. It doesn't even matter if you are right or wrong sometimes. The only option is to keep moving. That's how I do it. I'm trying to keep moving even if I don't know where the path leads. I used to know, at least I thought I did then." The tapping pen was only on Scout's side of the phone; he couldn't even hear Brenley breathing. He wasn't sure how else to explain his life—

"Some people think studying the past is useless. If I can see where the path started, the current path makes more sense to me. It's possible to see patterns and connections from a distance. Up close, those blur out of focus for me." Brenley rustled papers and sighed. "I think we both need to get more sleep."

Laughing, he picked up the phone and held it close. "Personally, I enjoy our drunken chats, Doc."

"Is that supposed to be more of your charm?"

"Touché. It doesn't make it less truthful. You've

helped me when everyone else is only trying to use me." He rolled his eyes and shook his head. "Yeah, this qualifies as drunken rambling so I'm going to hang up now. I'll be in touch later. Eat something and take a nap."

"Take care of yourself, Scout."

17

SCOUT BLINKED AT THE MONITOR MERE FEET FROM HIM. A quick glance around the room revealed the other students were quiet and the substitute teacher was on his phone. The words of the program speaker barely drained the refrain in Scout's head.

Xibalba…follow the Jaguar…Xibalba

Fear spiked his heart rate and sent a crashing wave of adrenaline racing through him. For a moment, he could only hear the roar of blood in his ears. He felt the heat radiating from his skin as if the sky had already managed to set him on fire. The world around him disappeared once again.

Xibalba…follow the Jaguar…Xibalba

A cool touch on his hand ripped Scout from the nightmare and back to the classroom. He jerked away then blinked as the girl next to him blushed.

"Can you pass the copies to me?" Her hands flailed in an aborted gesture before she looked away.

Scout glanced around the room again to find most were still watching the program. A stack of papers perched precariously on the edge of his desk. He gathered them and blinked to bring the words into focus. Class Assignment.

"Here – sorry about that." He took one copy and passed the rest to the girl next to him. She wasn't familiar to him, but he no longer felt the need to know every student. Her light brown hair was pulled back into a ponytail and freckles stood out against the pink still coloring her face. She kept looking at him as she sent the remaining copies to her other neighbor.

"No problem. Watching television is boring. I don't know why they force us to do this." She smiled and jotted a note on the top of her copy. "I'm Becky. I get extra credit for taking advanced classes."

"Advanced classes?" Talking to the stranger kept Scout from panicking about his nightmares moving from his sleep to his waking hours. "I'm Scout."

"Yeah, everyone knows you. I mean…I'm sorry…my mom says I need to learn to edit before speaking." Becky bit her lip and winced. "You aren't angry, are you?"

"How old are you?" He wasn't angry. His confusion grounded him further in the moment and helped block the hazy nightmare. The energy faded from his body and left a trail of goosebumps along his flesh.

Her head moved with her exaggerated eye roll. "I'll be fourteen this summer."

"You're in middle school, and you get credit for taking high school classes." He'd heard the teachers advising them of the visiting students, but Scout hadn't listened too closely. As most of his peers still ignored him, he expected the same from the younger kids. This girl had admitted she knew of him, but she wasn't running away screaming.

Becky doodled on the margins of the handout. "Yeah,

it'll help me get to the college classes offered here. If my calculations are correct, I'll have half of my general studies requirements when I graduate. If I get my bachelor's in—" She snapped her mouth shut with an audible click and shifted in her seat to look forward.

The program continued though a few students were ignoring it in favor of their phones. Becky was only quiet for a few seconds before looking at him again. Scout resisted the impulse to smirk at her fear. She was actually braver than his classmates.

"Sorry again. My mom also says I talk too fast and too much. I'll stop bothering you."

He grinned and watched her blush again. "No problem, Becky. Nice meeting you."

Scout returned his attention to the monitor. With only half of the class left, he was able to listen without losing his grasp on reality. He gave Becky another smile before darting from the class. Lunch meant a quiet table and a chance to breathe. The cafeteria noise normally annoyed him, but he was grateful for the distraction. It was one thing to have nightmares and get images when he touched the artifacts. It was an entirely different thing to see and hear things in the middle of a class surrounded by other people.

Benjamin slid into a seat across from him. The freshman tennis player remained committed to making the varsity team and Scout was the one he thought could help him. Somehow, the boy had become one of Scout's few friends.

"Hey, man. It is a lot more crowded with the middle school kids here."

"Kids? They're only a year younger than you, Ben." Scout rolled the apple off his tray and onto the table. The brown spots weren't appetizing.

"That year makes a big difference," Ben mumbled around a mouthful of tater tots. He swallowed several times and gulped half of his apple juice down. "Did you see the schedule for next week? Coach is starting challenges before the season even begins. I'm with the JV crew but I'm first seed."

"Keep your seed and you should be able to challenge the varsity alternates." Scout scanned the room when the noise level rose again. He smiled as Becky bulldozed through the crowds to head his way.

"Scout, can I sit with you? This is our first day, and I don't think they planned well. You'd think the organizers would've known our numbers and separated us into different lunches." She plopped down next to him and started picking at her food without stopping to breathe. "I thought the sixth graders were messy, but you guys are worse. Did you see that table? It looks like the pigs I saw on a farm once."

At the sudden silence, Scout glanced to the right and saw Becky staring at Ben. He turned to face the boy and introduce them but Ben's mouth was hanging open as he stared back at the girl. After only a few seconds, Scout tired of waiting them out.

"Ben, this is Becky. Becky, Benjamin. She's one of the middle schoolers you mentioned earlier. He plays tennis and wants to be the only freshman on the varsity team." Scout stood with his tray in his hands. "Get to know each other. I'm heading to the library to finish a research paper."

Neither one seemed concerned about his departure. Scout chuckled and disposed of his tray. He moved toward the door, but stopped when he heard a crash. A group of seniors were howling with laughter, which wasn't unusual; the smaller boy scrambling to pick up the scattered food at their feet was. Scout prepared to turn away when he recognized a fellow tennis player, Brody Floyd. The senior kicked a fruit cup. Fruit pieces coated the younger boy, who had been reaching for it. The laughter grew louder as Scout drew closer.

Swift kicks to the closest chairs created space for him to reach the boy. Another kick toppled Brody. He cursed and knocked a friend down in his efforts to stand quickly to face Scout.

"What's your problem, Ainsley?"

Ignoring the question, Scout gestured to the kid. "Get out of here. The food's not worth it."

The boy's head bobbed up and down before he left without a word.

"I asked you a question."

Scout was still planning to walk away. The meaty hand around his arm made him pause and smile. The rush of blood again filled his ears with crashing waves. Black spots danced on the periphery as his vision narrowed on the threat. Right-handed – leaning forward – wide eyes. Heat spread through Scout's body. He settled lower and prepared to strike the enemy.

"Mr. Floyd, Mr. Ainsley. Do we need to meet in my office to discuss anything?"

Straightening, Scout turned to his principal as the waves of anger quieted. "We could." When Brody paled, Scout paused to grin. "I think that would be a waste of your valuable time, sir. We've finished our discussion and I'm leaving."

"Mr. Floyd?"

When Mr. Richmond spoke directly to the other senior, Brody shook his head and looked away. His ears were tipped red, but he didn't argue. The table of his friends also remained quiet.

"Okay then. I'll follow you out, Mr. Ainsley. The rest of you clean this up and get to class on time."

Scout wasn't surprised when the older man moved to his side in the nearly empty hallway. He continued forward at the same leisurely pace.

"I saw what happened. While I appreciate you protecting our young guest, I wouldn't appreciate having to suspend you for starting a fight." Mr. Richmond clapped a hand on Scout's shoulder and stopped walking. "You're very close to graduation, and you've put in a lot of work. Don't let anyone or anything stop you now."

"I plan to keep moving forward, sir."

Mr. Richmond squeezed his shoulder then dropped his hand. "Good, good. You do that."

Scout watched the principal leave and took another deep breath. "The problem is that my plans rarely work."

"How's your day been?" Leyna sidled up to Scout's side and smiled.

He jerked away from her and glared. "What did you hear?"

"Nothing, but now I'm curious. What's your problem?" Leaning against the row of lockers, Leyna watched him.

Scout stuffed new books into his bag. The lunch drama had followed him for the rest of the day. He could feel teachers and students watching his every move. It was too similar to his initial return from the Island, and it made him just as irritable. He was ready to go home. "Nothing. Have you seen the kids visiting for those advanced courses?"

"Did you argue with kids?" Her brow furrowed when she scanned the hall. "I don't understand the problem."

"There's no problem – just making conversation." Slamming the locker shut, Scout turned away from her. "You got any updates?"

She grabbed his arm and stood on her tiptoes. "Thomas is ready to meet. We can drive to the park right now."

"Sure, let's go." He adjusted his bag and made a beeline for the closest parking lot exit. Despite glaring, everyone scrambled out of his way. Scout threw his bag in the back seat while Leyna slid into the passenger seat. Neither of them spoke until he'd pulled out of the parking lot.

"Are you sure you're okay? You seem a little tense." Her hand hovered in the space between them before returning to her lap.

Keeping his eyes on the road, Scout tried to relax his grip on the steering wheel and breathe calmly. "The nightmares have been rough lately. I'm still not getting as much sleep as I need. Sorry for being an ass."

"Hey, no worries. I am sorry for you. Is it still the cenote dream?" Leyna reached out again and didn't stop until she rubbed his arm.

"I can't always remember them. Sometimes, it's memories of the Island." It wasn't technically a lie. He risked a glance to the side and smiled. "Thank you for setting up the meeting with Thomas."

After squeezing his arm, she clasped her hands together and stared at the road ahead. "Do you think we should mention the dreams to Thomas? They know more about the orb than we do. Maybe strength, speed, and healing aren't the only known things associated with it."

"I'd associate war and death with it." Scout realized he'd mumbled the words aloud when Leyna gasped and clutched his arm again.

"Would you really? What about—"

"I don't mean literally. I only meant that it was on the Island and that's what happened to us." He peeled one hand off the steering wheel to scrub over his face. "Did any of your tutors have you read *Lord of the Flies*?"

She released his arm and shook her head. "No. Should I read it?"

"It was an assignment for us last year. Just imagine war and blood but with kids. Maybe it's human nature, I don't know." A memory sparked in his mind – Gerard. *This world is destroying itself. If you believe mankind deserves a chance, you should team up with us.* He could see the Island after one particular battle – the street had been a mess of debris and bodies. The memory faded to a black and white blur then snapped back into focus. Bright red blood stained the pale faces frozen in screams of pain by their untimely deaths. He didn't know all of their names, but he knew the pain of surviving Atlantic Island.

"…I mean we don't really know what the Owl might represent."

Scout pulled his thoughts from the past and found Leyna staring at him. He could only recall a few of her words. When he didn't reply, she continued.

"Brenley mentioned wisdom and even clairvoyance for the Owl. What if somehow it can…"

"It can mess with your head? Drive you crazy?" Snarling the words, Scout shook his head and stared at the road. Anger again beat a fast, heavy rhythm in his heart.

"You know I didn't mean it like that. I think we need information on it, and Thomas may be able to help us."

"As I don't have the Owl, I don't see how it could make me any crazier." Scout glanced at the white of his knuckles during the awkward silence that followed. He peeked at Leyna and saw her staring at him as she twisted the bar in her ear.

"You really are having a bad day, aren't you?" Sighing, she shifted in her seat. "I'm definitely the person who understands how it feels when others think you're crazy. I know what it feels like for your family to think you're evil. I didn't mean anything about you when I asked about the Owl. My research has been all dead ends, and I guess I don't handle being scared that well. I also don't like feeling useless. Can we agree that we're both having bad days and let it go?"

A flash of fire then ice sliced through him. The pressure returned like an iron fist clutching his chest. Orange spots flashed in the periphery and—

"Scout?"

Leyna's voice sounded much closer. He turned and found her face inches from his. Brown eyes were dark swirling pools that grounded him with a comfortable warmth. He took a deep breath then another one.

"I don't want to ask if you're okay, but I am worried." Leyna's lips were tight and tucked between her teeth. She leaned back and stared at him.

"I'm sorry. Yes, we've both had a bad day, and we can forget it." He moved one hand to rest on her thigh. "I am sorry. I guess I really do need to get some sleep. You think the Turtle can heal something like nightmares? Maybe it can help with mental problems."

She sputtered a laugh and rolled her eyes. "You don't have mental problems or, at the least, not any more than I have."

"I'm not sure that's comforting, witch." Scout smiled at the return to familiar teasing. His heart rate slowed and the heaviness in his chest eased enough to make breathing easier.

"Funny, soldier boy." Her hand landed with a slap against his arm. She gave it another squeeze before pulling away. "Is there anything you want to share with Thomas?"

Deflecting, Scout shrugged then shot her a look. "Is your research really not going well? Is there anything you think we should share with him?"

"I found some stuff, but Brenley would have to decide what's important. There are a lot of theories interpreting the Mayan culture. Did you know the first researchers thought they were peaceful? That was before all the human sacrifice information came out." She shuddered then looked out the window. "We're already here."

"Perks of living in a small town. You're rarely more than twenty minutes away from anything. Let's see if Thomas knows anything. He's had time to study the Jaguar test results."

She shut her door and looked at him over the car. "You know he's going to want follow-up tests, right?"

"That's why I didn't bring either artifact." Scout smirked and winked at her. "Come on, let's go meet the leader of the Multiversal Monitoring and Enforcement Agency."

Laughing, Leyna walked to his side and linked her arm to him. She hummed softly as they walked. Scout felt another burst of anger and looked away from her. His heart again raced as energy filled him. Red and orange colored his world. His thoughts frayed as the buzzing in his head grew loud enough to overwhelm Leyna's song. He clutched her arm and forced himself to speak.

"Do you think Thomas would offer you a job after you graduate? I don't know what degree you could get for time travel enforcement, but I've seen you fight and that has to count for something." Scout tried to picture Leyna during their sparring. With her next to him, her scent of flowers and spices fueled the memories. He took a deep breath and stared at her.

"I don't...I've never thought about it like that." She looked up and away several times before tugging him forward.

Her words pushed aside the encroaching images, but not the anger. Scout hadn't intended to confront her. Lying by omission was something he had almost convinced himself he could forgive and forget. With anger heating his blood, he couldn't stop himself from pushing. "You really should think about it. It'd allow you to use your unique skills. Plus, I'm sure he could use your help."

He breathed through the blood rush and tried to focus on Leyna's response. She was staring into the distance. The awkward silence did little to reduce his anger. Her shoulders moved in spastic circles and her head jerked to take in every direction. After a silent minute, she nodded and pulled him to a stop. She lifted her chin and met his gaze.

"Scout, there's something I need to tell you."

When she didn't immediately continue, he stepped closer. "Okay, go ahead."

"I think I've waited too long to speak up, but it never felt like the right time. That's what I've told myself, but I'm not sure you'll see it the same way." Her gaze fell then flicked back up to him several times. "I have thought about working for Thomas after graduation. And not just because I have a unique skill set as you said."

The anger swirled in a turbulent whirlpool in his gut. It wasn't a nervous fluttering of butterflies but more of a terrifying pterodactyl rave at a dance club. He wasn't sure what to say if she admitted the truth.

"I know you doubt him, but I do believe Thomas tries to do what's best. He didn't want the residents of Atlantic Island to die. He doesn't want Hodges' supporters to destroy this world either."

"Leyna is right about that, Scout."

19

Spinning to face the voice, Scout stared at the head of the MMEA. Thomas stood several feet away wearing his standard dark suit and tie. His brown hair looked windswept, but the beard and mustache were neatly trimmed. There were still soft lines around his eyes even though he wasn't smiling.

Glancing from one to the other, Scout nodded and offered a hand to the man. Leyna moved closer to Scout's side with a smile.

"Scout, Leyna. I'm glad we could meet."

"Thanks for making time for us." Scout smiled to balance out the snide tone he couldn't hide. He wanted Leyna to finish her confession; he wanted answers. Unclenching his fist, he allowed her fingers to intertwine with his. The harsh anger softened when he clasped her warm hand. "We're hoping you have some answers for us."

"Answers? I'm not sure about that. Things are changing, but we don't have that many answers."

"Did your tests on the Jaguar reveal anything?"

Leyna leaned toward the man but didn't release Scout's hand.

Thomas scanned the empty park then took a seat on a nearby bench. "Less than we'd like. It's made from obsidian. The eyes are stone covered in gold. It was created in an accepted Mayan style and dates back to that time. We could find no source of power, and there are no options to aid in searching for the other artifacts."

Scout released a disappointed sigh. He noticed Thomas watching him – the man was almost unnaturally still.

"It would help if we could test it again and the second artifact. A Turtle, correct?"

"The Turtle is made of green jade, which was commonly used by the Mayas." Scout supplied the details without blinking or offering to supply either artifact.

Thomas glanced once at Leyna then slumped back against the bench. "Did the archeologist provide that information?"

"Yes." Scout refused to answer more than the question.

The leader of the MMEA gave him a small nod; Leyna muttered and squeezed Scout's hand hard.

"Brenley has helped us, but we don't want her to be in danger because of that. Can you keep her out of the official reports?" Leyna released Scout's hand and crossed her arms over her chest as she stared at Thomas. "If you want her to continue to help, she needs to feel comfortable with us."

When the man didn't immediately agree, Scout couldn't stay quiet. "She needs to trust us. She also needs to stay alive and free."

"Okay then. We'll do it that way," Thomas conceded

and did another visual search of the area. "Scout, can I ask you some questions?"

Looking around the park himself, Scout breathed deeply before answering. "Sure, ask your questions."

"I don't think you appreciate being called an anomaly."

At the man's pause, Scout rolled his eyes. "If that's a question then no, I don't appreciate it."

"Fair enough, but that doesn't mean you don't have special skills, possibly even more than you are aware of currently. There is one theory that perhaps you aren't the only anomaly. There could be other people who may also have certain, shall we say, unusual abilities."

Scout stepped closer as his questions tumbled out. "Why do you think that? What abilities? Were they on the Island too? Where are they now?"

Holding up his hands, Thomas waited for Scout to snap his mouth shut. "We are working on theories to explain some ripples in the Prime Universe. I think we told you previously that we aren't Traveling much right now. A universe can sustain a certain amount of human interference and survive. However, the Atlantic Island merge took a toll on the Prime Universe. We aren't sure if the ripples are a result of that or something new."

"And those ripples have given some humans abilities? Are they like Scout?" Leyna pressed for details while Scout remained silent.

"We don't have any answers. We do have a lot of theories and rumors." Thomas stood directly in front of Scout. "Have you felt anything strange? Anything that reminded you of Atlantic Island? Has anything changed for you recently?"

Scout wanted to believe Thomas was good; he wanted to believe in the man and in Leyna. Acting on that belief was difficult. He tried to balance out fear with hope and stay in the middle. "I've had unusual nightmares lately. I don't know what they mean. Dream research can't agree on how to explain human dreams. Desire, firing neurons, cataloging memories. There's no agreement by the experts and therefore no way to interpret dreams."

Thomas blinked and frowned. Scout felt his face flush once he realized he had shared information gained in therapy. He'd read the research from Dr. Wake during one of the many nights he couldn't sleep after a nightmare. He plunged ahead before either of them could question him.

"They sometimes start in a cenote and we've researched that connection. Leyna, you should send him your notes on Ek Balam and the White Road." Before she could reply, Scout looked back to Thomas. "They sometimes start on a beach like the Island. I can't always identify the location. It's like the real world has merged with the fictional nightmares."

"Maybe the worlds are merging." Thomas turned away to stare at the park before he took his seat again. "I have more questions."

"How about we ask some first?" Scout didn't sit down, but he did move to the other side of the bench. It gave him more space between him and the enigmatic leader. "Are Hodges' supporters causing trouble?"

"What kind of trouble?"

Scout frowned at the request for clarification. His strategy to be vague and get information he didn't know he needed wasn't starting off well. "Trouble meaning people are dying."

Thomas rubbed the bridge of his nose then nodded once. "Yes, people have died."

"But collateral damage is the price of war, right? The price of power?" Scout stopped short after taking a step closer to Thomas. He saw Leyna shifting her weight from side to side but he didn't meet her eyes.

"It is the price of war as I'm sure you know. That doesn't mean those fighting want it to happen. I didn't want anyone else to die." Thomas stood and turned away. His hands were jammed into his pockets and his shoulders pressed closer to his ears.

The blood rush passed as quickly as it had come. Scout slumped down onto the bench when his legs trembled. He waved off Leyna's concern and cleared his throat. When Thomas turned to face him, Scout didn't look away from the penetrating stare. "You're right. I didn't want all of those people to die on the Island, but I couldn't seem to stop it either. It didn't matter which side I was on."

"You didn't fight with Theo and Kylee?" Thomas made no effort to close the distance between them.

"No, I didn't." Scout saw the flash of knowledge across the leader's face and looked away.

"You fought for—"

"Yes." Scout didn't allow him to finish the question. He glanced up to see Leyna's apparent confusion. His lies of omission were worse than hers. "They recruited me from school, and it made sense to follow those orders. I have regretted that choice many times."

"So has Tiberius."

Scout flinched at the words. He hadn't heard the Supreme Leader's name for months. He'd heard it too much in the beginning and then again when he'd joined the Sons of Tiberius. A hand on his shoulder forced him up to his feet. Thomas again lifted his hands before he stepped back.

"I'm sorry for what happened to you on Atlantic Island, Scout. I'm sorry your life hasn't returned to normal."

"I hear normal is relative so it's no big deal." Scout shrugged off the concern. "Is there anything you can tell us about Hodges and what's happening?"

"Is there anything we can do to help you?" Leyna breathed out the words in a rush. She pursed her lips when she looked at Scout. "That doesn't mean we can do what you ask, but I'd like to know if you think we can help."

Thomas looked from Leyna to Scout, then sat again. "I understand you don't want to give up the artifacts, but it would help us to test them. We know there are people who want them; you've met a few already. We do not know how they plan to use them. The artifacts aren't the only battle we're facing either."

Scout stayed quiet and was grateful Leyna did as well. Thomas seemed to be weighing his options and considering his strategy. When the leader started speaking again, Scout felt the tightness in his chest ease.

"I can't tell you much about the other battles. I can tell you we don't want anyone other than you to get the artifacts. I'm still hopeful you'll trust me, Scout. Until then, I might be able to provide some help. We've been tracking some known supporters of Hodges. They've been in Mexico as you have. They have also Traveled to Europe."

"Europe?"

"What?" Leyna's yelp was much louder than Scout's question.

"We haven't been able to locate Hodges' intel on the artifacts, but someone in his organization must know something about them. However, you still seem to find them first, and that's a very good thing." Thomas smiled then stood once more. "I'll send you the information we have on their trips. Perhaps, it will make more sense to you than us."

Swallowing fast to conceal his gasp, Scout stood as well. He offered a hand once more.

Thomas accepted the handshake. "I'm trusting you. I hope you'll keep in touch and trust me too. I don't want to see anyone else die."

20

Scout watched the MMEA leader until he was no longer visible. Leyna's shuddering sigh pulled his thoughts from past battles and those still to come.

"What do you think happened?"

Turning to face her, he watched her jerky movements as she looked around the park. He scanned the area once again too. "I think people died on his watch. I also think that's probably why no one is coming after us. They want all of the artifacts, and it is easier to let us find them." He didn't share the rest of his thoughts on the easiest way to get the artifacts from him.

"Died?" Leyna's mouth opened and closed several times before she nodded. "I'll send him the research I have. Whatever he sends us, I'll forward to Brenley."

Scout watched her for a second longer. "Thank you."

"Well, yeah, it's not a big deal to send notes." Leyna looked around again. "We should probably head back. Do you want to visit Brenley this week?"

"I meant thank you for trying to protect Brenley. I know you don't trust her—"

"That doesn't mean I think she deserves to die," Leyna interrupted.

"I get that. You didn't have to fight for her protection though. I didn't even think to mention that, but you did. Thank you." He leaned in slowly. When she didn't pull back, he kissed her. "Thank you."

She rested her hand over his heart. "It wasn't a big deal, but you're welcome." Leyna grinned before pulling his head down to kiss him. "You're welcome, partner. Now, let's get out of here."

They were both quiet on the short trip but did exchange more kisses before she went her own way. Scout didn't want to dwell on love or war, but he couldn't stop his mind from replaying the conversations with Leyna and Thomas. The pressure returned to cinch his chest in a tight grip – his heart raced and his breathing became shallow. Picturing Maya in vivid detail, he counted his breaths until they were slow and steady again. He swallowed hard and picked up his phone to call Brenley as he drove home.

"Did Thomas have any information?"

"How did you know about the meeting?" Scout's thoughts turned to betrayal and fear, but Brenley's chuckle mocked his panic.

"Leyna sent her notes to me and asked that I review before she sends them to Thomas. She said he was also supposed to send us something. It was logical to conclude you had met with him."

"Okay, yes, that's logical. We appreciate the help." He pulled into the driveway and looked around before getting out. "How is the research going?"

"Not as well as I'd like. We are looking for evidence to support our theories. Scientists should look for theories to explain the evidence they have."

When she paused, Scout could picture the furrowed brow and tight line of her mouth. "Well, you've got the degree. If you think we should try something else I'm game." Opening the front door, he put his bag down and shifted the phone to pick up Maya. "Hold on, Brenley."

"Anyone home?" Scout paused to listen but didn't hear anything. "Yes, Maya, I know you're here. We'll go out the back and work out. Come on, let's go."

He stopped for dog treats and continued to hold the squirming dog. Once outside, he gave her one treat then threw a tennis ball across the yard for her. "Sorry, Brenley. I wasn't thinking when I called you. I have to play with Maya."

"You have a dog named Maya?"

Scout rolled his eyes at the carefully blank tone. "Yeah, I do. Sue me. Let's get back to business then I need to go. I can call you back tonight."

"What business?"

"You think we're going about this the wrong way. You'll have to tell me what the right way is. I've been making it up as I go." Patting Maya, he bounced one ball on the patio then sent another flying. She barked before grabbing the closest one and dropping it at his feet. Without waiting, she raced to find the second one.

"I'll think about it."

He wasn't surprised that was all she offered. "No one will ever accuse you of being overly chatty, will they? Okay, Doc, think about it. I'll call you tonight."

"Goodbye, Scout."

Tossing the phone aside, he caught Maya as she jumped into his arms. "Good job, girl. You ready to work out?"

He set up the course and started their training. It helped clear his mind and work off some energy. By the time they'd finished, he was covered in sweat and Maya panted at his feet. Brenley's comments continued to demand his attention even after a hot shower and real food. His parents had returned but only stopped by his room for a few minutes. He had his phone out as soon as they left.

"Scout."

"Yeah, Doc, I have an idea. We've told you our thoughts and ideas and you've joined our team. But, I think you have a good point. This isn't how you normally do things."

"I want to help you." The tapping had already started on her end.

"Now, who's jumping to conclusions without all the information?" He laughed then laughed harder when the tapping grew louder. "You don't put a sharpshooter on the front lines. You don't put a field medic with the cooks."

She didn't speak, but he was sure he could hear her gritting her teeth.

After another long pause, Scout put her out of her misery. "What I mean is that we need you to do your thing. For you to be at your best, you need to do it your way. Not mine. So, if this was your problem to solve, what would you do?"

This time the silence was comfortable. Scout stretched out on the bed and patted Maya while Brenley considered his words. He already knew she worked at her pace and only shared information when she felt it was right to do so.

"I want to focus on Dacey. He was the one who called you the Guardian of the artifacts. He also had one in his possession. Like you, he is connected. The rest of us are following you." She issued a soft sigh then the tapping resumed at a slower pace. "I have his paintings so that is where I will start. The way to know Dacey is to know his art – that's something I do remember. I will also visit his house again."

She didn't offer a logical reason for the visit, but Scout didn't press her. "Then do it. You need to be careful and maybe get off your usual path a bit. If anyone is watching his house, they will recognize you." He had to hope Thomas would try to keep the archeologist safe as they'd requested.

"You are the one who should be careful. Without Dacey, you're the only living connection to the artifacts, and everyone involved knows this. However, I will be smart. I will also review Leyna's notes and whatever she sends." The tapping noise paused then resumed at a quick pace. "Did Thomas mention anything that concerned you?"

Scout hesitated to speak of war, even if Brenley saw skeletons every day.

"You either need to tell me or your therapist."

Barking out a short laugh, he rolled his eyes. "Yeah, okay. He spoke of people dying."

"People die every day."

"When you feel responsible for their deaths, it's a little harder to accept that truth." His head hit the headboard when he closed his eyes and leaned back. Maya adjusted to cuddle closer to his side.

"I'm still getting used to the idea that you were a soldier for ten years. I knew you weren't a normal high school kid, but that apparently didn't prepare me. I apologize."

"No worries—I still struggle to get used to my life too." Scout appreciated the snort of laughter on the other end. "Enough about that, you start doing things your way first thing in the morning. You need to get some sleep right now."

"I will if you will." There was a rustle of fabric before it was quiet again. "Rest well, Scout."

"Sweet dreams, Doc." Scout clicked off the phone and plugged it in to charge. He slid lower in the bed and curled on his side to face Maya. "Wake me up if you can, girl. I think it's going to be a rough night."

His nightmares were battle scenes from the Island. It wasn't hard to understand the meaning of the images – he knew what a commander meant when they said people die. Bodies, burnt and twisted, scattered over the beach. In the blink of an eye, he teetered on the edge of the cenote filled with skeletons.

Scout fell backward and felt the sharp pain of new injury. Blood flowed from the slice across his palm. He stared at it then balled his fist to stanch the flow. The scratch of falling rocks pulled his attention back to the cenote. He saw only the flash of a young girl moving with more speed and grace than any adult soldier on the Island had.

"Galaxi. Is that you?"

No one answered. A flash of white-hot pain rippled across his hand. He looked down at his hand again; the wound was now only a thin red line along his palm. There was no pain, only a pulsing warmth battling an icy chill. Scout scanned the area, but there was no sign of Galaxi or any other human. He noticed a paw print in the mud as a buzzing sound started soft and low. Too soon, tremors rocked his body and dropped him to his knees.

The blue jade owl and the patient white snake,
Hunt together during the night,
Prey for prey,

The circles of life rarely ever break,
Destiny is your own to create

The sweet melody broke through the haze of pain. Scout gasped for breath and slowly sat up. He was back on the beach alone.

Xibalba...follow the Jaguar...

He woke up with a start and Maya still curled peacefully at his side. Scout rubbed the grit from his eyes and slid from the bed. He ran a hand over the dog's side. "I'll be right back."

After gathering his laptop and notepad, he returned to the bed. He couldn't shake the idea of people Thomas knew dying. A few broad searches brought too many results and no comfort. Checking the phone, he gave up the idea of calling Brenley.

"It can't hurt to try her way."

Scout spent the rest of the night listing the 'evidence' they'd compiled so far. He didn't try to organize the information; he only wanted to try and see it in a new light.

21

"IF WE FOLLOW THE EVIDENCE—"

"How exactly do we follow evidence? This isn't a crime drama. We're talking about…" Leyna stopped whispering even though none of the other students in the hall were watching them.

"Talking about time-traveling witches and crazy twenty-something soldiers masquerading as normal high school students?" Scout chuckled and handed her a piece of chocolate. "It's Brenley's idea and I guess it's that whole scientist thing. She said we were trying to find evidence to fit our belief or something. I'm only trying to look at things in a different way."

Munching on the chocolate, she shrugged. "Okay, what evidence are we following?"

"The Jaguar." Scout closed his locker and started toward the library for his free period. Leyna dogged his steps with an annoyed sigh. He made her wait until they were in the media room to continue. "I've always heard follow the Jaguar, only now I also get Xibalba."

"The place of fear, the Underworld - yeah, I've read

about that disturbing place." Leyna polished off her candy and leaned against the work station. "How are we supposed to follow the Jaguar?"

Scout dropped his eyes to the ground. "Yeah, that's the part I haven't figured out yet."

"What *have* you figured out?"

When he didn't reply, Leyna grabbed his arms. Scout tried to ignore the pink flush crawling up his face.

"You haven't figured out anything, have you?" She rolled her eyes and paced the length of the small room.

Scout didn't argue, but only because he had no logical arguments to make. After reorganizing his notes, he hadn't been able to find another way to look at anything. The voices and images in his head weren't exactly evidence that could be used in court against Thomas or the rogue agents. They could be used as evidence to get him institutionalized, even if he hadn't been entirely wrong.

"Okay, obviously, Brenley should do her thing her way. This though" –Leyna gestured between them– "this has been working pretty well. We've found two artifacts. I think we should keep doing what we've been doing."

She accepted his silence as agreement and unpacked her stuff. Scout leaned against the wall closest to her and rubbed a hand through his hair. The lack of sleep made it difficult to think, much less win an argument against Leyna. He swallowed the sudden need to laugh but couldn't help smiling as he watched her. Her movements were always fast; they were rarely smooth or soft. The witch had a toughness he couldn't help but admire.

"Okay, here we go. I've sent our research to Thomas and he provided the travel spots connected to time travel activity. As the Travelers aren't his people, we have to assume they support Hodges."

Placing his hands on Leyna's shoulders, Scout studied the map she brought up. There were several dots in different colors. "I'm going to need more coffee to understand the significance of this."

She smiled and put one of her hands on his. "It's not a lot yet, but it may be possible to find a pattern in their movements. That could tell us more. It may even link to something Brenley discovers."

"Let's do this – give me some names and I'll start checking." Scout moved to the right and slid into the seat next to Leyna. "I do have to leave early today. I have an internship interview. Coach got my teachers to agree to let me skip so I could be at practice. We can train after that."

"Why do the kids in the movies never have to worry about school when they are saving the world?" Leyna bumped her shoulder against his and grinned. "Here, you can have the last bite of chocolate since you look so pitiful. Where's all that charm now?"

The chocolate was sweet so he ignored her teasing. After washing the treat down with water, he pulled out his laptop and nodded. "Hit me."

Leyna rattled off a list of cities and dates. She also noted which ones had multiple activities.

"Wait, how do you spell Bilbow?" Scout paused and studied his typing. "I'm pretty sure my version isn't correct."

"B-i-l-b-a-o. It's in Spain."

"Got it, thanks. I'll start there. Let the fun begin."

The quiet was punctuated only by their typing for several more minutes.

"Barcelona is known as the Holland of the South – there are hundreds of cannabis clubs." Leyna rolled her shoulders back then hunched over her screen again.

"We should add Barcelona to our travel list then. London might be fun too. Big Ben isn't the name of the tower, but the clock inside. You know, in case you were wondering." Scout winked then returned to his computer.

Thirty-five minutes later, they'd found nothing useful. They had kept each other entertained with facts about the cities they were researching. Scout pushed away from the table with a groan.

"You know another thing those hero kids don't have to deal with?" He didn't give her time to guess. "Sore muscles from research."

Leyna chuckled but stood and stretched as well before putting away her stuff. "You're out the rest of the day, right?"

"Yeah, interview, tennis, and then I'm all yours. I have a test to study for tonight so we might need to push through a faster session. We could do the playground again."

Groaning, she still nodded. "Okay, but I get to pick the first course."

"Works for me." Scout leaned in for a quick kiss just as the door opened. He jerked back to face the intruder and felt himself blush under the librarian's gaze.

Mrs. Morrison stood tall to look down her nose at Leyna. She pushed the door open and moved to the side. "Mr. Ainsley, Coach Martin asked that I remind you of your appointment. I believe you need to be leaving."

Leyna rolled her eyes and pushed by the older woman before turning back to grin at Scout. "I'll see ya tonight, baby. Be ready for some fun."

The Librarian drew in a quick gasp. "Ms. Carlyn, that is hardly appropriate behavior."

Leyna waved over her shoulder and practically

pranced away. Mrs. Morrison turned back to Scout and he bit the inside of his cheek to keep from laughing. Widening his eyes, he gave her an apologetic shrug. She softened but didn't speak.

"Yes, ma'am. I'm going right now. I have an interview at the museum for an internship this summer." He added the details in hopes of remaining in her good graces.

"That would be an excellent use of your summer, Mr. Ainsley. I wish you luck."

"Thank you, Mrs. Morrison. I'll be sure to let you know how it goes." Scout walked sedately across the library feeling her eyes on him the entire way. He closed the door and sprinted down the hall with a laugh.

He skidded to a stop when the hall blurred and tilted before his eyes. He wasn't as surprised as he thought he should be when he imagined Dacey standing at the far end of the hall. Slowing down, he even nodded to a few students racing to their classes. He waited for the hallucination to fade, but it didn't. The man in front of him smirked and held his gaze.

"I've really gone crazy, huh?" Scout kept his focus on the hall instead of the figment of his imagination. "You can't be real. This doesn't make any sense."

"I'm not a ghost." Dacey laughed and leaned closer. "You won't turn to stone if you look at me either."

Nodding to Ben, Scout was glad the freshman continued down the hall. "I thought I saw you because I had the artifacts and was standing over that weird stone in your back yard...what is that thing anyway? I didn't think I would see you again."

"You've seen me since then." Dacey moved to stand in front of Scout.

"That was a dream." Scout watched as the artist

shrugged but didn't offer any additional information. "I thought I was dreaming."

"Again, I'm flattered you dream of me, but we don't have time for that right now. Why haven't you gotten the Snake? Dawn will be breaking soon."

"And that's why we don't have the Snake. What does that even mean? Dawn will be breaking soon?" Like steam off the asphalt on a summer day, a pulse of energy blurred Scout's vision. He pivoted and slammed a fist into the closest locker. Rage burned through his gut to spread fire through his body. Drawing back his fist again, he froze when he felt Dacey grab his wrist.

"That's why you need to find the Snake. Without all of the artifacts, the power is unbalanced. It will kill you."

The pressure on his wrist disappeared as Dacey let go and stepped back. Blinking quickly didn't keep the other man in focus.

The blue jade owl and the patient white snake,
Hunt together during the night,
Prey for prey,
The circles of life rarely ever break,
Destiny is your own to create

Pain shot through Scout's head when the world snapped back into focus. There was no evidence the artist had just stood before him. Rushing to his car, Scout fumbled with his phone.

"Scou—"

"Did Dacey ever paint any scenes of the dawn?"

"I don't know. That's not what I—"

"Find out." Scout threw his backpack in his car then slapped a hand against the vehicle's roof. "I'm sorry, Brenley. Could you please see if Dacey referenced the breaking dawn in his art?"

"Yes, of course." The archeologist paused then almost whispered her next question. "Are you okay?"

"I have no idea. I'm running late for that internship interview. I'll call you later." He didn't wait for her response. Starting the car, he slammed it into gear and sped from the parking lot.

ARRIVING ON TIME AFTER SPEEDING THROUGH TOWN, SCOUT smiled at the museum attendant. "Hi, I'm Scout Ainsley. I have an appointment with Mr. Pendergast."

"Sure, he's on the second floor. The elevator is right through those double doors."

"Thanks, appreciate it." Scout let his gaze roam around the large space as he walked. The building helped distract him from thoughts of war and insanity. There was a large aquarium in the middle and a candy shop on the left. There were smaller doors and hallways along the right side. He barely glanced at the exhibition posters as he continued forward.

"Scout Ainsley?" A middle-aged man looked up from a messy desk with a smile. He stood tall and wide enough to tower over Scout when he offered a hand. "Good to meet you, son."

"Thank you, sir. I appreciate you taking the time to talk to me." Scout looked Mr. Pendergast in the eyes and clasped his hand.

"You're right on time, but I'm running a little late. How about we grab coffee and move to a conference room?" Navigating his large frame from behind the desk, Mr. Pendergast knocked over a stack of papers when he reached for a folder. He twisted to see the damage and knocked a football helmet off the desk.

Scout caught it and offered it back. "Don't want this getting damaged."

Chuckling, Mr. Pendergast placed it on top of a file cabinet. "That's evidence of my past glories. We definitely don't want anything to happen to it. I already cracked the glass case, and I doubt the Missus will want me to spend more money on it. I wore that during the state championship senior year – everybody from our team signed it."

Keeping his face serious, Scout slid back a step to allow additional room as the man recounted the tale of a football game from decades earlier. The story continued as they poured coffee and took their seats in the cramped conference room.

"Pardon the mess. We're in the midst of the fundraising campaign and need every flat space to mail out flyers and thank-you notes. Of course, the notes contain an easy way to make another contribution." Mr. Pendergast pushed the small table closer to Scout and give himself room to sit.

"My parents enjoyed the dinner. My mom was particularly excited about your plans." Clasping his hands together, Scout rested his forearms on the table. He looked around the room while the older man shuffled through the papers in the folder.

"Got your papers in here somewhere. Your mom was a very nice lady. Your father secured matching funds from his company. Ah, here we go. Scout Ainsley, eighteen, graduating this year. Good grades, tennis captain. Nice record. Of course, tennis isn't my sport." Mr. Pendergast pulled additional pages out and made two stacks. "You're interested in the business internship so you won't be working on the exhibits. We prefer college kids with an interest in history for those positions."

"I understand, sir. It is the marketing and administrative side that interests me." Scout repeated the words he often used when talking to his father's friends.

"Is it now?" Mr. Pendergast peered at him under bushy brows before turning his attention back to the folder. "Your teacher recommendation noted you have a new interest in history."

Scout wondered if there was also a note from Dr. Wake. He kept his smile in place and knew it was time to lie. "History is a new interest. Even you've just admitted the importance of business savvy here in the museum. Marketing and administration experience would be useful regardless of my college degree program."

"True enough. I didn't understand that when I fell into working with the city and then the museum. I didn't have a plan past high school myself." He shuffled more pages then placed a notepad on top of one stack. "Now, I know I have a pen here somewhere."

Scanning the room didn't reveal a pen, but a framed picture caught Scout's attention. He stood to read the words at the bottom.

"That's the Guggenheim Bilbao. Have you been to those museums? The buildings themselves are works of art. I got to visit the one in New York as part of a training program. It inspired our newest building, and I shouldn't have to tell you what a controversy that stirred up in town meetings." He shuffled the papers once more.

"Now, let's talk about this internship program and see if you're a good fit for us."

Scout fielded the questions with ease. He hadn't needed to get a job yet, but he had shadowed his parents on many meetings and events. There was always a flow to conversation and that was easy to find with the museum coordinator.

He left Mr. Pendergast smiling as he gave the promise that he could accept the position if they offered it to him. Scout's smile faltered when he returned to his car. There was no time to ponder Dacey's words or appearance. There was still tennis practice and Leyna to face before he could return home to again evaluate his sanity. His phone beeped the notification of new messages, but he ignored them.

Tennis helped him worked off some of his bad mood. The spring season hadn't started, but Coach ran them through drills to improve stamina and speed.

"Jog a lap then come back here. Save that strength and breathe. We're running suicide drills next."

The chorus of groans and curses only made Coach Martin laugh.

"The more you complain, the more we do."

Scout pushed Ben into line in front of him. "Move it. Shut up, guys. Let's go." He wasn't as winded as the others, but he refused to consider if Leyna was right about lingering effects from the artifacts. He'd barely broken a sweat.

"I guess our captain has spoken. Everybody fall into line like good little girls."

Twisting to look back, Scout gave his fellow senior a long look. "You've gotta run off that Christmas candy sometime, Brody. You've put on a few pounds."

"I can still kick your ass, freak." The brunette player

allowed friends to hold him back, but he didn't stop running his mouth. "Shouldn't you be strapped down in a padded room somewhere?"

"Don't put your BDSM fantasies on me, man." Jogging backward, Scout winked at his laughing teammates. The anger filling his body was more of a comfortable warmth. It even allowed him to breathe easily while the others were gasping for air.

"You stupid son of—"

"Scout, I've got a date with Becky this Friday." Ben's overly loud voice cracked at the end. He flushed a brighter red when the other guys laughed.

Jumping in before the locker room commentary could start, Scout sped up to nudge the smaller boy with his shoulder. "Race ya, Ben. Think you can keep up?"

They finished in first and second place, but Ben was bent over at the waist and unable to stand tall in the victory. Scout slapped him on the back with a laugh. The others joined them in much the same state as Ben.

There was no time to rest or argue before Coach started a series of suicide drills and volley exercises. Everyone collapsed on the court once Coach blew the whistle for the last time. Scout had won all three rounds, but it had meant he was hot and sweaty even with the cool temperature.

"Hit the showers and head home. Remember to submit your grades next week. If you don't make the grades, you don't make the team. We have tutors available…"

Blocking out the coach's words, Scout pulled himself up and kicked Ben's leg. "Let's go, kid. You've gotta pick up the balls before you're finished."

The other players abandoned the court at his words

as he'd known they would. Scout offered a hand to pull Ben up.

"Seriously? I have to pick them all up."

"It's a matter of rank. If you want on the varsity team, you've gotta put in the time." Clapping a hand on the boy's shoulder, Scout laughed at his pout. "Grow a—"

"It's always good to see a team captain lead by example. Show Ben how it's done." Grabbing his clipboard and whistle, the older man smiled at them both.

Ben's face perked up at the words, but Scout only shook his head and reached for the closest ball.

"We'll see you in the locker room." Coach Martin walked away swinging the whistle from one hand.

"Scout, I'm sorry—"

"No worries. It'll give Brody a chance to cool off. It's all good." He also hoped it would help him stay calm. High school sports always included trash talk, even between teammates. He and Brody had been on the same teams their entire lives. They weren't friends, but they'd never been enemies either. "I'll take this side, you take that one."

They worked in silence for the few minutes it took to gather the balls. Scout looked at red color still staining Ben's face. As he watched, the boy opened his mouth to drink then breathe.

"I thought these weren't real workouts. This kicked my butt."

Scout couldn't agree with him – he felt great. His muscles didn't feel like jelly as they had after other practices. He'd already cooled off and no longer felt sweat dripping from his face. "They only get harder, but that's how you get to play with the big boys."

Ben rolled his eyes then glared at him. "How do you look so good?"

"You hitting on me, kid? I don't think Becky would appreciate that." Scout winked then laughed when Ben's face turned an even darker shade of red.

"No, that's not...I mean you're...I don't..." Ben continued to stammer even when Scout laid a hand on his shoulder.

"Just shut your mouth and breathe. You can't let a little trash talk get under your skin. It gives the other guy an advantage." Scout tugged him forward so they could walk to the locker room. "You've gotta laugh this stuff off and keep your head in the game."

"You mean like you—"

"Aren't you two a cute couple? I guess we know how Benny hopes to make the varsity team." Brody smirked as he twisted a towel in his hands.

Glancing around the locker room, Scout only saw teammates, not their coach. Most were trying to mind their own business, but a few were laughing.

"Hey Benny, if you're giving out free blo—"

Scout watched Brody's head bounce against the locker. He was the one leaning into the boy with one arm pressed against his throat. Eyes bulging, Brody stared at him. When Scout blinked, the roar of blood receded and he heard the calls of the other players.

"Get Coach!'

"What the hell happened?"

"Back off, Scout."

"Told ya he was a freak."

"Come on, Scout, let him go." Ben's words were softer than the others, but he was the one pulling at Scout's arm.

Turning, Scout looked at the boy then released Brody. The strike to his face would have been worse if Scout's instincts had been slower. He allowed himself to be pulled away without fighting it. Brody's arms swung wildly and connected with other targets as he tried to reach Scout.

A shrill whistle broke through the commotion and quieted the crowd. "Scout, Brody, in my office now."

2 3

Scout heard Leyna's approach but didn't turn around. He did fight off her hands when she tried to cover his eyes to surprise him. Spinning around with a hiss, he bit back the angry words when he saw her pale.

"What happened to you? Did someone hit you?"

"It's not as bad as it could have been." Scout grumbled and turned away when she reached for him. "Tennis practice got a little intense."

"I didn't realize tennis was a contact sport." Leyna moved to stand in front of him with her hands on her hips. "What happened?"

He wasn't ready to confess to his struggles and glared back at her. "The guys were picking on Ben. You remember him? Freshman kid who stuttered when he met you. Should I have let them kick his ass?"

"Of course not." Her expression softened a degree. "Do the other guys look worse?"

Snorting a laugh, Scout rolled his eyes and smiled at her. "Actually, no. I started with a choke. His was more of a lucky sucker punch when I released him."

She placed a hand over his heart. "Are you sure you're okay? Have you gotten any more sleep?"

"I'm fine. You got your course picked out?" He turned away to study the playground.

After pinching his side, she patted his chest and smiled. "I do. I even marked it."

"Marked the course? What do you mean?" Scout started to walk forward, but she stopped him by returning her hand to his chest.

"Nope, no cheating." Leyna brought both hands to his face and forced him to look at her.

Avoiding her eyes and lips, he focused on her piercing. The new brow hoop piercing was a fiery red.

"You know the order of a rainbow, right?"

"Roy G Biv."

"Good boy, that's right. Red, orange, yellow, green, blue, indigo, and violet. That's the color order for the flags and posters. Sorry, but I didn't think about this until a few hours ago so I couldn't get flags in every color. You're a big boy so you'll have to figure it out." Leyna continued to hold his face and grin. After a quick kiss, she pulled back. "Think you can beat my time, soldier boy?"

"That's hardly fair. You set the course up and—"

"Go!" Leyna turned him around and gave him a hard push.

Scout didn't waste time glaring at her. Scanning the park, he spotted a splash of red on the far end. He sprinted forward while still looking – the yellow and blue flags were easy to find. After running along the seesaw, he spotted an orange poster board. It took little time to climb up the super dome. The vantage point allowed him to see the green flag.

"Roy G Biv." Scout half slid down the dome to run to the yellow flag at the monkey bars.

The rope wall had the green marker and the blue was attached to the swing set. Smirking at Leyna, he jumped over each swing before touching the flag.

"What are you waiting for, soldier boy?"

"Roy G Biv." The words were a reminder to him as he scanned the area once more. A hint of purple caught his eye and he rolled his eyes. She had marked the far end of the small treehouse. They hadn't played on it last time since he was much bigger than the normal-sized child.

Leyna's laughter followed him as he bumped and slid down the slide. Legs on the ground, he had to land his knees to get his whole body out of the tunnel. He ignored her laughter and looked for the final flag. It was tucked along the edge of the sandbox and rested on the ground. Scout ran forward and dove over the box without injuring himself.

"Ha, I bet you didn't think I could do it." He slid to a stop and grinned down at her.

"Technically, you didn't do it." Leyna laughed hard enough to have to lean against him to hold herself up.

After giving her a couple of seconds, Scout sighed. "I did do it. Roy G Biv – I hit every obstacle."

"More like Roy G V Bi." She gasped for air and wiped a tear away as she continued to laugh.

"What are you talking about, witch?" A pulse of anger mixed with need when she again pressed into his body. He could feel her smile when she kissed his neck. "Leyna."

"It's not my fault you're color blind. The sandbox is blue, the swing is indigo, and the slide is violet." After sharing that information, she collapsed against him with laughter.

"Okay, okay, whatever. I still did it all. And now, I get to move the markers before you race." He held her tight when she tried to fight the rule change. "Nope, it's only fair. Go stand by my car and look away. Can I trust you?"

Scout had meant the words as a joke, and Leyna took them that way.

"Yeah, yeah, I'll be a good girl even though you're a sore loser. I totally killed your time on my course." She kissed his cheek and strutted away, still chuckling to herself.

He was locked in place staring after her. The flare of heat was replaced by a chill down his spine. Scout flexed his hands and felt the fine tremor in the motion. Pushing down the emotional turmoil, he ignored the twisting ache in his stomach and planned his course. He was grinning when he returned to Leyna.

"Are you ready to play, witch?"

"I was born ready." Leyna laughed and linked her arm through his. "Is this the trash talk you have on the tennis courts? If so, I can see why you got punched. I have to confess I've felt the desire to do that myself."

Scout lifted his brows and widened his eyes innocently. "Is that all you've felt the desire to do to me?" His wink made her laugh.

"Always the charmer, but I'm still going to win this round. Then we'll see who gets to give in to their desires."

"Deal." Scout grinned and covered her eyes. "Fair is fair, right? Keep walking straight forward." He deliberately pressed into her back with each step. If her quick gasp was any indication, it served to distract them both.

"You can stop now." He kept his hands in place and leaned in close to her ear. "Go."

Leyna stayed in place for a second after he had

spoken and removed his hands. The kick to his shin when she sped away made him grimace. She sped to the red flag and quickly found orange and yellow. Green proved more difficult, and she ran around in circles.

"Need some help?"

She ran by him, and Scout couldn't be sure, but it sounded like she cursed him. He laughed until she found the green marker. Blue was another easy one. Crossing his fingers, he watched her circle the playground again then once more. He kept his mouth shut even after she came to a stop and turned in a slow circle. She glared once at him before running to the indigo poster.

"Still got one to go, and time is wasting." He added a helpful gesture to his watch and could see her glare even across the park.

It took her several more minutes to backtrack and find the violet flag on the other side of the super dome where the blue flag was. Leyna managed to shake her head and frown as she ran back to him.

"You cheated!"

"You didn't say the flags had to mark different obstacles." Despite her annoyance, he pulled her into a hug. She was still shaking her head when she returned his embrace.

"Since you cheated, I won." Leyna pulled back to grin then leaned in to kiss him. "And to the victor go the spoils. I want to go back to the hiking trail with the scenic overlook. You have time to get us food, and we can enjoy the full moon tonight since there shouldn't be any clouds."

"It's going to be cold, and I don't have time to get a tent." He wasn't really opposed to the idea.

"I'll bring blankets." She hugged him again and snuggled close. "Don't you think I deserve a night off?"

"What about me?"

"I'm letting you be with me. How is that not a victory for you too?" Her lips twitched against his skin as she interspersed the words with kisses.

"When you put it that way, sure." Scout tugged her hair to get her to lean back so he could kiss her. "Give me an hour and a half. We can park at the overlook so it won't be a hike. The view will be great."

As they pulled apart, Scout felt the rush of cold through his body. He kept smiling until he was back in the car alone. Pulling the shirt from under his seat, he held the Turtle and Jaguar. He closed his eyes and embraced the rush of power, even as it came in a flash of fire followed by the suffocating pressure of a wave. The accompanying images brought no comfort – they did bring a dull throb to the base of his skull. After several minutes, he wrapped both up again and stuffed them under his seat. He couldn't explain the need to touch the artifacts often. He did hide his new habit from Leyna as they'd agreed to limited contact with them.

The lingering sense of emptiness followed him like a shadow as he prepared for another date with Leyna.

$$2 4$$

IT WAS EERILY SIMILAR TO THEIR PREVIOUS DATE, ONLY THERE was no tent, no snow, and Scout wavered between love and hate. The artifacts were tucked into the first aid kit in his car because he again gave in to the need to keep them close. He glanced back even though he could barely see his car through the trees.

"What's wrong? You keep looking back there. Do you see something?" Leyna pitched her voice low, but her short nails dug into his arm even through his jacket.

"No, it's nothing." Scout rubbed her hand then laced his fingers through hers. He sighed as he studied the beauty of her face. It was easy to lean in to kiss her; it was harder to pull back and focus on her real role in his life. "It's nice to get away from the research and training."

She used her free hand to move his face back to hers for another kiss. Her smile was soft as she gazed into his eyes. "You feel guilty slacking off."

"No, it's not—"

Leyna waved off his response. "Don't worry. I feel

guilty too. There's so much going on, and I keep thinking about people dying."

Scout moved them both to a new position so she could rest against him. "I know this wasn't how you imagined your new life outside the Fair would be. I don't think either of us should feel guilty about resting. It's required to keep your body and mind to peak condition."

"That sounds like the soldier talking." Leyna cuddled closer with a laugh. "In some ways, this is better than I imagined when I left Marcus and the others. In some ways, it's simply confusing."

Tilting his head, he could see her lips twist before she bit the bottom one. Scout felt the push to comfort her and the pull to confront her. "Yeah, I get the confusion thing. The Island was more black or white, live or die."

"I only know a little about Atlantic Island. I recognized the names Theo and Kylee. I also know who Tiberius is."

Again, Scout flinched at the Supreme Leader's name. Leyna rubbed small circles on his stomach and placed butterfly kisses on his neck.

"You don't have to tell me if you don't want to, Scout. I can't even imagine what you went through there. It must have—"

"Tiberius brought order and security at first. I was just a soldier doing what we were told to do. I thought it was black or white, live or die. Theo and Kylee were my age, but they didn't see it that way. They didn't follow orders. They led the Uprising." Scout cursed the fact that his memories hadn't faded. Even uttering the Supreme Leader's name brought a rush of painfully bright images. "I wanted to serve. I liked having a purpose. Things didn't improve, and we had to accept that the Island was our new reality."

Leyna continued to offer silent support with the soothing strokes sweeping down his chest. She didn't press for details, and he didn't plan to provide them.

"There was blood spilled on both sides. People died. Those who didn't, they wanted to."

She gasped then bit back additional noises to squeeze him tight. Scout let more memories pass through his mind. Hot, sunny days – gunfire at night – flashy government buildings – storms and death.

"The Uprising didn't solve the issues. There were more problems as the factions divided the Island. We exchanged one government for another. People still died." He'd watched from a distance as Kylee and the other leaders had changed over the years. He didn't like to think about how he'd changed in order to survive. "Then there were more rebels pushing for something different yet again. The Sons of Tiberius. It didn't matter what side you were on or what truth you believed – soldiers died, civilians died. The latest war had just ended when Thomas arrived to stop Hodges' planned destruction."

The colors of setting sun mixed with his bitter memories and brought out his nightmares. It was no longer his small town on the horizon below, but instead a Mexican forest. Scout breathed through the hallucination and hoped Leyna would give him more time. Her comforting hands felt miles away when the fading sun bounced off the Mayan pyramid to reveal a slithering snake.

The blue jade owl and the patient white snake,
Hunt together during the night,
Prey for prey,
The circles of life rarely ever break,

Destiny is your own to create

A pounding base continued after the soft melody and Scout's heart thudded in time with it. Fire twisted in his stomach as a chill caused him to hunch his shoulders.

Xibalba…Xibalba…Xibalba

Painted orange and pink by the setting sun, the snake continued down the pyramid. Scout wasn't sure if the darkness following it was feathers or shadows. He couldn't look away as the animal ended its journey by coiling next to a stone snake head. Heart racing faster, he tried to stay calm and still when the snake stared at him. Darkness fell over the image as an eerie silence descended. Reality returned with a sharp, piercing pain behind his eyes. "Reality, yeah."

"What?" Leyna tilted her head back to look at him. "What did you say?"

"Nothing." His shrug dislodged her head from his shoulder. Sitting up, he rested his arms on his thighs and directed his attention to the few remaining colors of the fading sunset. He turned back once more but ignored the forest to see the dark sky behind them. Stars were already visible in the east. "We've studied the constellations in class. The teacher even referenced Mayan uses of astronomy and astrology."

Leyna accepted the abrupt subject change without batting an eye. "I've read more since we discovered the Orion thing. I can understand why Brenley likes archeology. I've enjoyed what we've discovered…you know, except for the…"

"The voices in my head, Dacey's disappearance, and a possible war here." Scout nudged her shoulder and smiled briefly. "Fearing for your life does put a damper on the fun."

"It's not only my life I'm worried about, you know."

Leyna bumped him back and slipped her arm through his. "I know things aren't easy for you right now, but you need to take more breaks. You need to get some sleep."

"Come on, let's move back to the parking lot. It has a better view of the stars." After grabbing their picnic leftovers while Leyna rolled up the blankets, Scout offered his hand to her. "I have to say, I can't usually see the constellations. Orion's belt is pretty much the only one I can pick out."

"It does seem strange, doesn't it? The ancients had complete stories and connections to gods that meant so much to them. I look up and think it's beautiful, but all I see are white dots." She followed him to their new spot and arranged the blankets to her satisfaction before pulling him down with her and lacing their fingers together again.

Lying on a large rock, they studied the sky silently for several minutes. Leyna's giggles broke the silence, and Scout moved onto his side to look at her.

"I really don't see anything but polka dots." She continued to chuckle as she hid her face against his chest.

Scout grinned and pulled her closer to kiss her temple. He leaned back, but turned her around to face the sky. "Okay, hold on, I have an idea." He managed to pull his phone out without either of them having to move.

"Are you going to find out what we should be able to see?"

"Yes, because there's an app for that." He downloaded it and pointed his phone at the sky. Pulling it back down between them, they studied the results.

"Canis Major...oh, I can see that. It's a dog." Leyna sat up and looked from the sky to the phone several times. "What else?"

Smiling at her, Scout tried again. "Okay, that's supposed to be the Giraffe, but I don't know."

Leyna's face fell and her brow furrowed as she stared at the sky. She grabbed the phone and glared at it before trying again. "No, that's not a giraffe."

He pulled her back to lie down again and wrapped his arms around her. Her warmth and familiar scent wrapped around him and sent a tremor racing through his body. "How about we just enjoy the view?"

"Yeah, I can do that." She placed her arms over his and sighed. "It is a beautiful night even without snow."

The warmth was replaced by the icy press of an iron band around his chest. His breaths came in shallow pants as Scout struggled for control. That night had been magical and easy. At that time, he hadn't known she had lied to him. He hadn't known she had gotten close to him for her job.

"Hey, you're harder than the rock." She elbowed him, but didn't turn to face him. "And no inappropriate jokes."

Exhaling with a laugh, he dragged in more air and forced his muscles to relax. Leyna wriggled and took up the space he'd created.

"Much better, soldier boy."

The darkening twilight brought more stars. Silence settled over them with the darkening sky, comforting and soft. Without any additional hallucinations, Scout felt exhaustion pull his body into a deeper relaxation. Leyna shifted until she was facing him. Her soft lips traced random paths along his jaw and neck. Heat bloomed again, but it wasn't fueled by anger or fear.

She moved between his legs and stretched out on top of him. Scout opened his eyes to smile at her before she pressed her mouth to his. He ignored the past and future to enjoy the moment. His hands roamed under her jacket as hers slid beneath his shirt. The nip of her teeth brought the aching need into a sharp pain. He rolled her underneath him.

The ringing phone caused a cacophony of forest sounds to erupt around them.

Scout grabbed the phone without looking away from Leyna's flushed face. He planned to toss it aside until he saw Brenley's name. Leyna's brows rose when he answered the call.

"What's up, Doc?"

"I found a painting by Dacey called *Before the Breaking Dawn*. And that's not all I found. You and Leyna need to get here right now!"

"SHOW US WHAT YOU'VE GOT, DOC." SCOUT PUSHED through the unlocked door with Leyna on his heels. The archeologist had provided a new address for them to meet her. He glanced around the metal warehouse where the university temporarily stored its archeological records. Shrugging, he turned to the woman standing in the middle of it.

Brenley didn't even look up. "I found these glyphs hidden behind Dacey's art supplies in the storage shed. Aren't they beautiful?"

After a single glance at Leyna, Scout crossed the space to Brenley's side. The stone tablets were brightly colored and clearly in the Mayan style. Scout recognized the familiar image of the jaguar and snake. Leyna pressed in close to see the artwork, but didn't speak.

The archeologist blinked then looked at them with wide eyes. "I called you less than five minutes ago." Her hands flitted in the air before dropping to her side.

"The beauty of time travel, Doc." Scout smiled and nodded to the table. "Did you find all of this at Dacey's?"

Shaking her head in small jerky motions, the woman moved to the other side of the table. "Yes, I did. I'd been studying his paintings, but I knew something was missing. My notes had details on pieces I believe he did for us. Those were not as brilliant as these. This is what I imagine they would have looked like originally. Our science isn't advanced enough to fill in these details. This is art."

Leyna lifted a hand but didn't touch the pieces. "I've only seen the chipped, faded images. These feel alive."

Scout slammed a hand on the table after anger rolled through him in a suffocating wave. "Great, they're beautiful. How exactly does that help us? Your new 'follow the evidence' strategy was supposed to be better. It was supposed to give us answers."

Only the sound of his loud pants filled the room. Both women were staring at him, but Scout dropped his gaze to the table of art. The cheerfully bright colors mocked the darkness of his mood. Spinning away, he strode toward the door. There was no plan in his mind, only the splashes of oranges, reds, and blues ricocheting through his brain. No voices gave him direction or knowledge. He stood alone.

"Scout?" Leyna spoke from across the room but didn't add to his name.

Brenley's footsteps were loud thuds in the quiet space. She stopped several feet from him. "I'm sorry. I got distracted and haven't explained this well. These tablets have each of the animals represented and do provide some insights. No, they don't give a location for the Owl or Snake. I think they do tell us something new, something that will help us."

Dropping his head, Scout tensed to avoid the shaking he knew followed the oppressive rush of adrenaline and emotions. He ran a hand through his hair then lifted his gaze to meet Brenley's eyes. "You shouldn't apologize. I was being an ass."

Leyna's aborted laugh was poorly concealed by a cough. Scout spared her one glance before staring at Brenley.

"Seriously, Doc, this is all on me. I'm sorry. Please show me what you've figured out." The heat flowing through him was embarrassment, and even his ears felt hot.

The archeologist gave him a soft smile and motioned him forward. When he reached her side, she nodded once and walked with him back to the table. Brenley rearranged the glyphs while Leyna moved next to Scout.

"This is the order I found them in, but I don't think that is necessarily important. I've tried various combinations and think this one reveals the most to us." Making a lap around the table, she reordered the tablets and added the painting to one side. There was a single word written on a piece of paper below it.

Brenley studied the arrangement then picked up the piece of paper. "*Ahalcab* – Mayan for dawn or break of day. We don't need to worry about the full meaning. I think this was a message from Dacey." Placing it on the table, the archeologist turned back to look at Scout. She closed the distance between them. "You had me look into this. You asked specifically if Dacey had drawn anything relating to the break of dawn. Why did you ask that?"

Holding her gaze when he planned to lie was difficult. He avoided even glancing at Leyna. "I've seen Dacey in my dreams, remember? He said it to me."

"You've dreamed about Dacey?"

Scout smirked at Leyna's question. "You have a

problem with me dreaming about a guy? Does it help that the dream also included blood and pain?"

"I didn't mean it like that. I thought you'd said you'd been remembering the Island." Leyna snapped her mouth shut and winced.

He waved off her concern about sharing his secrets. "My nightmares are always evolving to include new horrors mixed with the old. Dacey was actually a nice change of pace." Scout turned back to the archeologist and found she continued to study him.

"The voices have not said anything new?" Brenley didn't blink to ask the question.

Rolling his eyes, Scout sighed. "You don't pull any punches, do you? And I know, that response doesn't make sense to you. I'm used to everyone walking on eggshells around me since they're worried about my sanity."

"I am worried about your sanity and your life. I'm also worried about Dacey." Brenley softened but didn't look away. "Have the voices said anything new?"

"I still hear Xibalba when the nightmares come." It wasn't a lie, but it wasn't the full truth either. He plunged ahead regardless. "As I've answered your question, can you get back to explaining all of this to us please?"

It took several seconds before the archeologist looked back at the table. "You found the Jaguar first then Dacey helped you get the Turtle. Your notes on the Turtle included a reference to Orion and Pleiades, Scout. Orion is represented by the turtle and Pleiades was drawn as a snake."

Scout nodded when Brenley paused, but he wasn't sure what else to say or do. Leyna bounced on her toes without interrupting.

"I used the order of Jaguar, Turtle, Snake, and Owl to set up the glyphs. In that order, we can see the story grow." The archeologist gestured to the table then pulled up her computer too. She even took the time to pull out a notepad. "I admit sleep deprivation could be responsible for this breakthrough, but stranger things have pushed science forward."

It was rare for the woman to ramble and Scout had to smile. "I think you must be a chatty drunk, Doc."

Brenley pursed her lips then turned back to the table. "Look at the background. Only the Jaguar has a night sky with yellow stars. The sky lightens for the Turtle, and it looks more blue than black. The Snake glyph has bright oranges and reds. The Owl is soft blues and whites."

"It's night turning into day?" Leyna posed the question as she bent over the Snake tablet.

"Couldn't it also go day to night?" Scout wanted to believe Brenley was on to something. He was tired of beating his head against the wall and failing. "You accepted my experiences as part of your hypothesis. Doesn't that impact your results?"

The archeologist stared at him for several seconds before a smile lit her face. "You have listened and read, haven't you? You're becoming a scientist."

"No, I'm not. I am desperate for answers, and you seem to be my best bet so I'm doing things your way." He rubbed at his neck and looked down at the table again. "Are you going to keep explaining this?"

"Yes, I am. Let's look at this new art that Dacey named *Before the Breaking Dawn*. The cenote represents the opening to the Underworld, which symbolizes the Xibalba you've heard. Look at the edge of the water in the center of the painting. There's a paw print."

"Jaguar." Leyna released the word on a soft sigh and touched the painting.

"I think so. There are the three rocks again – Orion for the Turtle. Despite the name, the sky above isn't a sunrise. We can see the constellation is the Pleiades, the Snake. That again gives us the order for Scout to find each piece."

"What about the Owl? Is it represented here?" Scout rubbed a hand at the corner of the canvas, not quite touching the paint.

Brenley frowned and shook her head. "Stay with me, Scout. There's more to Dacey's message than the order you've found the artifacts. There's you."

"What? I'm part of the message?" Scout stepped back from the table and the archeologist. "That doesn't make any sense."

"This painting is new and probably his last piece before he disappeared. He knew you had the Jaguar and he gave you the Turtle. This is a message to you and about you." Brenley tilted her head and peered at him.

Turning away, Scout didn't reveal that Dacey might be sharing messages with him since his disappearance. He wasn't confident enough in that new reality to share it. "I think you're right about sleep deprivation. You're grasping at straws."

"I don't think she is," Leyna disagreed. "The one thing Hodges' agents and Thomas agree on is you, Scout. You are at the center of this."

He turned back in time to see Brenley smile at Leyna. A warmth itched along his skin and made him twitchy. Scout tensed his body and remained as still as he could.

"The Mayas were among the earliest civilizations to use the concept of zero. Dacey knew this and I think he used you as the starting point." Brenley returned to trace a hand over the artwork. "Below the paw print is the symbol for zero."

"That circle with the lines?" Leyna lowered her head to look more closely.

Brenley pointed to the image of the scroll on her computer screen. "Yes, that's it. It's not the first time we've seen it. I should have noticed it, but we were more interested in the animals. It is at the center of the compass too."

Scout glanced between the painting and image of the scroll. The symbol was clear now that Brenley had pointed it out. He didn't understand the significance.

Her face softened for a moment before she nodded once and looked back at Scout. "You are at the center of this. To find the Snake, you must be in Xibalba."

"You want me to swim in a cenote? Sure, Doc. I can do that. Let's go right now." Scout saw Leyna wince at the sharp edge of his tone, but Brenley didn't flinch.

"You are taking the art too literally. Xibalba is your place of fear."

She continued to study him as if waiting for him to understand. Scout gritted his teeth and held her gaze. The edge of his vision darkened, but he didn't blink. The hum in his head grew into the familiar chant.

Xibalba…Xibalba…Xibalba.

He could see Dacey in his mind's eye. The artist lounged in his bedroom during what Scout had thought was a dream.

How hard is it it is to find your place of fear?

Brenley smiled when Scout's mouth fell open. The pieces clicked into place and silenced the voices. His place of fear was obvious. Laughter started soft and deep then rolled out until he bent in half. Leyna rushed to his side but didn't touch him.

"Scout, are you okay?"

He laughed harder at the absurdity of his life. He'd had the answer all along but hadn't seen it. Those in power hadn't seen it either. More laughter spilled out before he was able to breathe again. Standing upright, he smiled at Brenley and Leyna. "Yeah, I'm fine."

"Are you sure?" Leyna rested a hand on his back.

"As sure as I can be." He turned back to Brenley. "What else have you figured out, Doc?"

Leyna didn't give Brenley time to speak. Her hand clutched and pulled at Scout's shirt. "Wait, fill me in. I still don't understand what's going on."

Scout nodded to her then looked back at the archeologist. "The Snake was on the Island."

26

"HOW IS THAT A GOOD THING? WE CAN'T GET TO THE Island. I don't understand how this helps us find the Snake." Leyna paced around the table.

Scout wasn't sure why he thought it was good news, but he did believe it was. It didn't make sense that Dacey could visit him. Nothing in his life made sense. The Snake being on the Island was a solid lead. He had to try to find it. "It has to be a good thing."

Brenley moved to her laptop and clicked several times. "Leyna, stop pacing and come here. You too, Scout."

They moved to peer over the archeologist's shoulder to see a brightly colored flyer inviting all to an exhibit of Mayan artifacts in Atlantic City. Leyna pushed closer then sat down and started typing. Brenley stepped aside and Scout did the same.

"Your research connected me to the orb and Mexico in part through this exhibit, which I helped create. The orb isn't listed on any of the official records, which means they have been tampered with somehow. It is possible all records of the Snake have also been removed."

"Are you saying we can't confirm the Snake artifact was there?"

"We may not be able to confirm it, but it is a logical conclusion considering the evidence." Brenley looked away briefly then pursed her lips and met his gaze again.

"By evidence, you mean a painting and tablets from a friend we can't find? I'm not sure that's a convincing argument, Doc." He shook his head and turned away, only to have his gaze land on the table. His fingers twitched, but he didn't move closer.

Brenley stepped to his side and placed a hand on the Jaguar tablet. She lifted a brow and waited for him to do the same.

"Okay then." He placed his hand on the Turtle and waited. Nothing happened. "Nothing – no voices, no images."

"You don't look relieved," Brenley noted without judgment.

"Scout, care to guess where that Mayan exhibition has been displayed this year?" Leyna pushed away from the computer with a grin.

It took only a few seconds for Scout to understand her excitement. "Barcelona, London, and Bilbao?"

Laughing, Leyna leapt into his arms. "Yes!"

"I feel like I'm missing something now. How could you know the schedule?" Brenley strode forward to see what Leyna had found.

Scout kept his arms around Leyna but turned them both to face the archeologist. "When we met with Thomas, he told us they'd tracked some Traveling in those places. It wasn't his agents, which means it's the rogue agents supporting Hodges. No one knows what they're up to, but it seems like too big of a coincidence to ignore it."

After a second, Brenley nodded. "Yes, I agree with that conclusion."

Leyna froze then slumped against Scout before twisting to face him. "How do we steal an artifact from a museum? If it was easy, they'd already have it."

"I'm picturing black masks, jumping over laser beams, and a fast getaway car." Scout bit back more laughter since both women seemed lost in thought. He released Leyna and tapped a rhythm against his leg – fast and upbeat. Images of a beach along the edge of a forest filled his mind with a mix of sweet and spicy scents. The sun warmed his skin as he listened to the soft lapping of water against the sand. He wanted nothing more than to run for the sheer joy of running.

"Where are you going?"

Scout stood in the open doorway staring at the night sky. There was no beach in front of him. Stepping back, he closed the door and turned to them. It was Leyna who had spoken, but Brenley also stared at him. "Sorry, I don't know…" He shrugged to end the sentence.

Brenley immediately turned back to the computer while Leyna frowned at him. He smiled and walked toward her.

"Here's the schedule for the exhibit and the listed items." Brenley hummed softly then continued to type. "I think I see the problem."

"What is it?" Leyna and Scout asked in unison.

The archeologist barely spared them a look. "There is nothing resembling a snake in the collection. Whoever was after it must have hoped the artifacts were on a rotation. That would explain visiting various museums."

"Why would they rotate out pieces?"

Scout was wondering the same thing. He was also wondering why the sudden rush of happy energy was fading. Leaning against the table, he fought the urge to slide down to the floor to sleep.

"Every museum has different traffic flows and available space. It's not feasible to keep an exhibit exactly the same at each location." Brenley moved to her tablet and left Leyna to work on the laptop.

"Scout, sit down before you fall down."

The archeologist pushed a seat to him after delivering the order. Scout dropped down into it with a sigh. His body and head ached with a dull thrum each time his heart beat. He rested his head in his hands and closed his eyes. The conversation flowed around him, but he couldn't gather enough energy to listen to them.

It was the rise in pitch and volume that broke through and jerked Scout awake.

"You have made it clear you won't allow me to Travel. I will make this trip." Brenley stood next to her tablet and stared at Leyna.

"It makes no sense to waste that time. It gives them a chance to find it first." Leyna's arms were crossed over her chest as she bounced on her toes and stared back.

Rubbing his eyes, Scout pushed up to his feet. "Okay, what did I miss?"

When neither woman answered, he pulled both computers to him. Brenley's tablet displayed a private archeologist chat room of some kind. He turned to find Leyna exploring the Guggenheim at Bilbao. "I still don't see what's going on. Did you find the Snake?"

Leyna rolled her eyes before pulling the computer back. Brenley sighed and tapped her pen against her leg. Scout expected Leyna's behavior, but the archeologist was normally calm and quiet. He studied Brenley for another second.

"Okay, someone has to fill me in." Scout ran a hand through his hair and almost pulled it out when silence remained. He opened his mouth as Brenley started speaking.

"I think it's possible the Snake is being housed at the original museum that organized the exhibition. As I've noted, each stop could display different items. Some might never be deemed fit to be displayed. However, they would be considered valuable and protected. That responsibility would fall to the hosting museum."

"Even if that's true, the tour is wrapping up next week and any borrowed pieces will be returned. Hodges' men could have missed the Snake. You have a better chance of finding it, Scout, and I can take you there." Leyna managed to glare at him and Brenley.

Scout was trying to put the pieces together, but he didn't understand their anger. He scrubbed a hand over his face. "I think I'm going to need caffeine to continue this discussion. How about we—"

"We don't have much time and can't afford to waste any of it. We can leave now and search the exhibit first." The bite in Leyna's tone was sharp and challenging.

"We don't have time to make a mistake," Brenley countered. Turning away from Leyna, the archeologist faced Scout. "I want to be there with you, and I can help. I have contacts who would think nothing of allowing me to see the exhibit storage. This particular exhibit is at the Guggenheim Bilbao. It is public, crowded, and has security. You can't just pop into a building that has two hundred-sixty thousand square feet of space. Less than half of that is considered to be open to the public. Even you would struggle to find anything there."

Scout pushed his seat back and stood. "Okay. You've determined the Snake is at the Guggenheim then?"

Smirking, Leyna waved a hand toward Brenley but didn't answer him. He turned to the other woman to find her expression almost blank.

"No, we have not, at least not yet. I can request records, ask questions, and arrange a visit for us. Or, you can Travel over there and hope you stumble across it."

"Like we stumbled across the other two," Leyna retorted.

"Back to your corners. We're on the same team so let's figure it out." Scout glanced from one to the other, but neither appeared happy. "Brenley, reach out and see what you can find out about visiting. Leyna, see if Thomas can confirm any trips to other museum cities."

Leyna rolled her eyes then frowned. "What are you going to do?"

"After you take us home, I'm going to sleep. You ladies look for your answers your way, and I'll look for them mine." He wasn't surprised when both stopped to stare at him. He rolled his eyes that the first thing they agreed on in the last several minutes was annoyance with him. "I'm only half joking about that. We do all need some sleep."

Within minutes, they stood next to Brenley's vehicle as she loaded up the last of the items she claimed she had to have. It had taken them two trips to get everything. She closed the door and looked at them again.

"And you'll go back through time to when you left?"

"We're trying to make as little a ripple as we can. We avoid people and don't Travel far." Leyna looked to Scout and twisted her earring. With a sigh, she turned back to the other woman. "Thomas believes time travel should be limited right now. Saving Atlantic Island might have messed up our Universe. We need to be careful."

"Thomas wants to save this Universe, but you think Hodges wants to reset it somehow." Brenley stepped closer to Scout and paused to study him with a frown. "You don't trust anyone and believe everyone is lying."

He could feel the tension radiating off her in waves, but her face cleared to a blank mask. "You need some rest, Doc. It's one thing to hear about this all and another to live it. There are still too many times that I don't understand what's happening in my life. Get some sleep." Scout moved forward to give her a brief hug. She remained stiff but did pat his back before he pulled away.

"Sleep will make everything better?" The quirk of Brenley's mouth revealed she was teasing.

Scout tossed his head back to laugh out loud. "Absolutely not. However, at least you'll feel better able to handle the craziness."

27

Days later, Scout had a moment between insults to suspect he wasn't handling the craziness well.

He stared at Brody's red face and smirked. His team-mate lowered his head and plowed forward. The boy's shoulder slammed into Scout's stomach and knocked him into the fence. The chain links curved backward under their combined weight. Scout held on to his attacker—a knee to the face gave him the advantage. He pushed the senior away, but Brody took Scout with him when he fell.

They grappled and rolled along the tennis court – neither gaining the upper hand. Their teammates cheered and the circle of excited spectators closed in tighter. A tennis racket to his head left Scout dazed. Brody rolled them over once more to land on top. A dull thud accompanied each punch to Scout's ribs.

Grunting, Scout struck up with the heel of his hand. Brody's head snapped back. Another push and Scout was free to roll away and stand. Blood dripped from the other boy's nose; tears welled in his eyes.

The crowd grew silent when Coach Martin and Mr. Richmond pushed through.

"No one moves. Don't even breathe." Coach Martin looked at each boy before looking back to the principal. "You should take Brody and Scout. I need to talk to these guys before I join you."

Mr. Richmond's face was set in a dark scowl. "That works for me. Five feet apart unless you want an immediate suspension and rescission of all college recommendations." He strode away without looking back to ensure they obeyed.

Scout grabbed his gear and followed the principal. His breathing was calm enough for him to listen for Brody to attack again. Behind Scout, the senior was breathing hard and cursing under his breath, but he made no attempt to continue the battle. There was no noise from the other players or their coach as they left the courts.

No one witnessed their procession through the halls and into the principal's office.

"Take a seat, gentlemen. I'm using that term loosely considering your behavior." Mr. Richmond sat behind his desk and folded his hands. He remained silent for almost a full minute. "I'm aware of your previous conflict, but Coach Martin assured me nothing else would happen. You've made a liar of him."

Brody barely grunted a response from his slouch in the visitor chair.

Shooting a quick frown at the boy, Scout sat taller in his seat. "Coach did warn us, sir. It's not his fault."

"Is that so, Mr. Ainsley? Whose fault is it?" Mr. Richmond leaned forward to rest his elbows on his desk.

"He's the freak who's always running off at the

mouth." Lips curled back, Brody jabbed a finger at Scout. "You aren't the captain, and you don't deserve to be."

"That is my decision, not yours." Coach Martin stepped through the doorway. He nodded to the principal. "I believe I've found your volunteers for the roadside trash pick-up. I haven't yet decided if they should wear orange jumpsuits."

"Excellent. I'll update Mrs. Ashby to let her know the next month is covered. Now, the question is what do we do with these two?"

Neither man spoke for several seconds. Scout kept his back ramrod straight and stared forward. He heard Brody shift and kick the table between him.

"I'd like for us to speak to them separately."

Scout saw Mr. Richmond nod his agreement with the coach's suggestion. There was another long pause as they made them wait for further instruction.

"Mr. Ainsley, outside please."

Standing, Scout nodded once and left without a word. Before he closed the door, he heard Coach Martin begin.

"Mr. Floyd, we can invite your parents…"

Scout walked to the edge of the main office. He rested his back against the wall and took several breaths. There'd been no mad rush of emotion or even hallucinations. He had listened to Brody smart off one too many times and had decided to shut him up. It had been intentional to force the other senior to attack first. An offensive strikeoften worked well on the battlefield, but not in a court of law. No one had died today, and no one would. It was unlikely they'd get more than a slap on the wrist for their behavior. It was a calculated risk Scout had chosen to take.

The problem wasn't with his plan. The problem was why he'd felt the need to plan for Brody's downfall at all.

He closed his eyes and tried to enjoy the silence. No kids in the hallway – no voices in his head. After only a few seconds, he was thumping his head lightly against the wall to count the passing seconds. It took entirely too many before he heard the door open. He snapped to attention and stared straight ahead.

Coach Martin walked out with Brody trailing him. His teammate met Scout's gaze and sneered. It wasn't hard to lip-read the insult. With Coach's gaze trained on him, Scout kept his expression neutral and moved to allow Brody to pass. He didn't even grunt when the boy's elbow slammed into his side.

"Mr. Ainsley, come with me."

Scout closed the door behind them. His coach was leaning against a bookcase while Mr. Richmond remained seated in the plush leather office chair. He didn't take a seat, but neither did he look his principal in the eyes.

"Have a seat, Scout." Mr. Richmond leaned back and shook his head slightly. "We have worked with your parents and doctors. I think we've been very accommodating. Don't you?"

Sitting on the edge of the guest chair, Scout nodded. "Yes, sir."

"Is there something else you think we could've done?" Mr. Richmond asked after a moment's pause.

"No, sir."

"We want you to succeed." Coach Martin rejoined the conversation. "I didn't lie to you, Scout. You've overcome a great deal and that is something I respect."

"It's something *we* respect," Mr. Richmond corrected.

He pushed the chair back to stand and moved to the front of the desk.

Scout leaned back to keep more space between them. They were being gentle as he'd suspected when they hadn't spoken to them together. Time travelers considered him gifted; normal people thought he was weak, broken. Scout still wasn't sure what he believed.

"You'll be graduating soon unless you pull more stunts like this." There was a new edge to Coach Martin's voice.

Blinking, Scout turned to look at the man. Mr. Richmond picked up the conversation.

"Why did you do it? Even at the start of the school year, you avoided physical confrontations. Why now?"

He wasn't sure he had an answer for himself, much less them. His mouth quirked as he decided on a portion of the truth. "Brody and I used to run in the same circles. I've always known he was an ass, but now I'm older and I have less patience for him."

Coach Martin was the first to break. His laughter rang out as he slapped a hand against the desk. Mr. Richmond sighed then smiled.

"Patience and wisdom are supposed to come with age, Scout." The principal glanced at the still chuckling coach before addressing Scout again. "You'll be on cleanup duty with the others. You'll also work weekends at the museum. They need volunteers right now."

"The museum?" Scout watched Coach Martin straighten as Mr. Richmond lifted a single brow. Both men looked smug. It was Scout's turn to smile. "Yes, sir. I'll work at the museum."

"Good, glad this has been settled. I'm ready to go home and have a drink." The principal grabbed his briefcase and keys. "One last thing, Mr. Ainsley."

Scout froze with his hand on the door and looked back.

"In addition to patience, you need to learn the value of trust and mutual respect. We aren't your enemies. Not everyone in this world is out to get you." Mr. Richmond studied Scout for several seconds. "We're here if you need us."

"I wouldn't be much of a coach if I didn't understand teamwork," Coach Martin added as he crossed the room and clapped a hand on Scout's shoulder. "Even captains need friends. There's nothing wrong with asking for help."

Scout looked from his coach to his principal. He'd expected little punishment due to his unique situation and his parents' influence. He hadn't expected gestures of respect and friendship. "Thank you both. I'll remember that."

"You do that, son. Now get out of here and rest up. Training doesn't stop just because you earned more work."

With a final smile, Scout walked from the room with his head up and his mind surprisingly calm.

2 8

It was almost time for his nightly call with Brenley when Scout's phone rang. He smiled then frowned at Leyna's picture on his screen.

"What's up, witch?"

"And hello to you too." Leyna's laughter was almost drowned out by a siren. She paused to let the noise fade. "Thomas has confirmed there was another trip. It just so happens that it was to another city with a special museum exhibition. I think it's time for us to make a move."

"Did you tell him why we wanted to know?' Scout lowered the phone and clicked the speaker on. He glared at Leyna's image.

"Of course not. He also didn't ask because he is trusting us. He's trusting you."

"Okay, I'll update Brenley."

"That's it?" Her tone seemed more puzzled than annoyed. "Are you okay?"

Scout smiled and tried to lighten the mood. "That's number four hundred fifty-seven."

"Four hundred fifty-seven *what*?"

He laughed when she took the bait. Scout could picture Leyna rolling her eyes. "Four hundred fifty-seven times you've asked me if I'm okay."

She groaned then chuckled. "Math isn't your subject. I don't really trust your counting skills."

"How about we change the subject?" Scout sat on his bed and lifted his free arm so Maya could snuggle next to him. "What's your museum heist plan?"

"Is that what we're calling this? I was thinking of something more like Project Slithery Swoop. Maybe Operation Traveling Thieves?"

He barked a laugh loud enough to make Maya join him. "Slithery Swoop? I'm not calling it that."

"Hissing Heist?" Leyna offered with a giggle.

"No, absolutely not." Scout listened to her amusement and grinned. "I hope your actual plan is better than the names."

"You're the soldier. I think strategy falls to you."

"We're definitely screwed then." He cleared his throat and kept the conversation moving forward. "I'll update Brenley, but we do need a plan to steal the Snake if it's there. I think you're right that we need to move now. Let's hope the Doc got some information too."

"Yeah, let's hope." Shuffling noises punctuated the silence following Leyna's quiet agreement. "I want us to work together. I know you trust Brenley."

He waited, but she didn't add anything to the thought. He glanced at the clock. "It's time—"

"Scout—"

They both stopped speaking and chuckled. Scout rubbed at the back of his neck when an awkward silence fell.

"You first, witch. You're older after all."

There was a rough edge to her laughter. "It's nothing. What were you going to say?"

"Not much – it's time for me to call Brenley. I'll send a message if she has anything to report. You need to be thinking of better names if I have to do all the planning."

"No promises, but I'll try."

"We can't be partners if you don't pull your weight." Scout rolled his eyes then shook his head. There was no need to reassure Leyna. However, that is what he was trying to do. "Sweet dreams."

"I wish you the same." There was another awkward pause that lasted a little too long. "Good night, Scout."

"Good night." Scout stared at the phone even after it went dark. The sadness causing an ache in his heart was somehow worse than the recent anger. He rolled his shoulders back and rubbed a hand over the scar on his chest. Memories of Leyna doing the same made him stand and drop his hand.

Maya scrambled to her feet with a soft growl. Her head then tilted to the side when she stared at him.

"Sorry, girl. I don't really have an explanation. I think you're the only one who doesn't expect one from me. You're definitely not the only one I've been apologizing to though. I may need to start carrying more chocolate with me to offer each time I annoy someone."

He pushed the dog lightly to resume his seat on the bed. Resting against the headboard, he pulled his notes and tablet out. The phone rang as he reached for it. "Hey, Doc."

"The exhibit is likely to contain the Snake artifact even though it isn't specifically mentioned. I've reviewed personal site notes from my contacts. The exhibit includes pieces from several sites..." Brenley paused to take a deep breath. "Some pieces were discovered in

Chichen Itza before I arrived there. I think there's a strong enough connection for us to visit."

"Okay, I trust your conclusions even if I don't understand them. Leyna also got confirmation that more Travelers have hit another city on the exhibit route. You said it was likely in storage, right?"

There was only a brief hesitation before she answered him. "Yes, at the Guggenheim Bilbao. I have been researching, and this particular exhibit contains several resin pieces from—"

"What is resin?" Scout wasn't surprised she'd already lost him.

"In this instance, it refers to copal resin. Blood of trees. It was used—"

"Blood of trees?" Graphic images of the human sacrifice filled Scout's mind. "Great, that is bound to add to my nightmares."

"Tree sap, Scout. It's not real blood. The Mayas used it as incense, as a binding substance, and for small figurines."

"You could've led with that, Doc." Scout rubbed a hand over his face and the back of his neck.

"You could have waited until I finished instead of jumping to conclusions," Brenley countered.

Scout bit back a laugh at her lecturing tone. "My apologies. Please continue to educate me."

"I will send you some research for you to review." The fact that she waited several seconds to continue spoke to her annoyance at his teasing. "Copal artifacts have been found in Chichen Itza and other Mayan ruins. It is believed resin incense may have been used as a cleansing ritual. It has been discovered at burial sites."

"To summarize, the blood of trees is associated with fire and death. Oh yeah, I'm excited to find this artifact."

Scout added the notes, even knowing Brenley's summaries would be more logical and accurate. "We'd thought it would be more about speed like the super soldiers on the Island. I guess this is another example of jumping to conclusions."

The archeologist sighed. "It is difficult and unwise to speculate at this time. We should stick to the evidence." She cleared her throat and shuffled papers before the familiar tapping started. "We have discovered associations with dawn, and death can be symbolic of a new beginning."

Rubbing at his eyes again, Scout leaned his head back and let his thoughts drift. He didn't filter the words. "Didn't the Mayans believe death was simply a transition? The Underworld is a few levels in their multi-layer view of the world. It's not the same as the Judeo-Christian view of heaven and hell."

"Those are popular theories. Studying the past is difficult as so much has been lost. We also cannot separate ourselves completely from what we study. Current philosophies and advances are always changing us and how we see the past." The tapping that followed was slow and steady.

Scout listened to the beat and closed his eyes. More thoughts tumbled out. "The Jaguar is South and associated with power, kings, and gods. The Turtle is the West, longevity or more precisely healing. East is the Snake – a new beginning, a cleansing, possibly fire. That leaves us with the Owl, which we know even less about. Wisdom. Clairvoyance. Messengers."

Brenley continued the gentle beat without speaking.

"All points around a compass. Balanced. Even. Powerful." Memories of Dacey's words flickered, but Scout continued his stream of consciousness rambling.

"The orb took us to an alternate reality, another plane of existence. Another level. There was no balance, no peace. The weather. The battles."

Nightmares and memories merged and twisted in his head. Bloody red splashing along sandy beaches – orange fire brightening a cloudless sky – a black night spotted with yellow stars. Crashing waves roared in Scout's ears.

"Scout!"

"I'm here." He answered automatically as he blinked and looked around his room. His harsh pants made his chest ache. Snagging his water bottle, he gulped some down then took another breath. "I'm here, Doc. I was just thinking about those glyphs and Dacey's painting."

"You were talking, but then you were almost singing. What was the song?"

A tremor shook his body. Sitting down, he ran his hands through his hair and stared at the Jaguar and Turtle artifacts he'd apparently pulled from their hiding places. He didn't remember taking the action. "I don't know. It was only random thoughts."

"I don't think it was. You said something about a Snake and creating your own destiny." Brenley's tone was soft, controlled.

"You don't have to baby me, Doc. I told you – I have a therapist. It's not like you to play so nice."

"I'm not being nice. I'm trying to get answers. Isn't that what we both want?" There was a metallic clang in the background, followed by rustling paper. "We agreed to work together. However, you are withholding information. I cannot provide assistance if I do not have access to all of the information. I'm trying to help you. You must always remember that."

His hands were rough when he ran them through his

hair. He slid to the floor next to the bed. Maya joined him immediately and they both looked at the artifacts. Scout placed a hand on each one. The familiar melody filled his mind and allowed him to share the words. "The blue jade owl and the patient white snake, Hunt together during the night, Prey for prey, The circles of life rarely ever break, Destiny is your own to create."

He released them and leaned back. His head flopped back to rest on the mattress, and he stared at the ceiling. Scout waited for Brenley to stop typing.

"Do you know where you heard it?"

"The same place I heard Xibalba." Scout didn't move even when Maya climbed onto his lap. His eyelids were too heavy to push open.

"In your head." The typing continued, but she didn't ask any more questions. "You need to get some sleep so do not check the files I'm sending until tomorrow. Scout, I need you to agree to this."

"Fine, whatever." He noted his words were slurred, but he didn't care. Slouching lower, he curled slightly on his side.

"Good night. I'm hanging up now."

He didn't hear any other words. The phone slid from his hands as he again heard the crashing of waves on the beach.

29

SCOUT'S NECK POPPED WHEN HE ROLLED HIS HEAD TOWARD the beeping noise. He turned the phone alarm off, but didn't move otherwise. When Maya's tongue rasped against his free hand, he plopped his hand on her head for a lazy scratch. Reality came back in stuttering revelations – the Guggenheim, the Snake, Brenley.

Grabbing his phone, Scout checked for messages and calls. Brenley and Leyna had sent information after his late-night call with the archeologist. He covered his face with both hands and took several breaths. More details rushed back with painful clarity. Brenley had accused him of withholding information.

"I'm lying." Scout lowered his hands and looked at the Jaguar and the Turtle. "It's not simply withholding information."

"Scout? Are you awake?" A soft knock followed the question.

Scrambling to his feet, he moved toward the door as it cracked open. The smile on his mom's face slipped when she looked at him.

"Did you sleep in your clothes?"

"I was working on a project and fell asleep while trying to figure something out. I did get a lot of work done." The new lies left a foul taste in his mouth. He turned away and rubbed a hand across his face. When he turned back, his mom held the artifacts.

"Is this another history project contest? You certainly have embraced the museum internship, haven't you? It is a wonderful opportunity and so much more than we'd expected. I'm not sure it will be as beneficial as marketing, but I think it will be good for you." She held one artifact in each hand. Her smile remained when she glanced down at Maya. "Good morning to you too. I can let her out while you get cleaned up."

Scout sprang forward to claim the artifacts. They were warm to the touch, but no voices or images distracted him from staring at his mom. "These are artifact replicas. Impressive, aren't they?" His voice cracked on the last words, forcing him to clear his throat.

"I prefer museum pieces that contain diamonds and sapphires myself." She patted his cheek. Her eyes never left his to even glance at the Jaguar and the Turtle. "Get cleaned up, sweetie. Maya, let's go."

The dog trotted along after her while Scout remained frozen for several more seconds. Replaying the scene in his head, he hid the artifacts once more then headed to the shower. It was later than normal when he reached the kitchen and he still hadn't reviewed the messages from Leyna and Brenley.

"Did you at least sleep well?" His mom handed him a cup of coffee and a green smoothie.

"Actually, I did. I guess I needed it." He patted Maya's head before drinking his breakfast.

"You're working too hard. Are you sure you have time for this new museum project?"

He glanced up to find his mom standing by the kitchen sink. She was focused on watering the herbs instead of staring at him. Breathing a little easier, he finished off the smoothie. "We've already had the push for college applications, but it's not time for graduation. Classes are slow."

"I can't believe you will be heading off to college this fall. I still remember bringing you home from the hospital wrapped in that blue blanket. You were so tiny and pink. You had—"

"Mom," Scout interrupted with a groan. "Can we not relive that moment again?"

She tried to tousle his too-short hair then settled on kissing his cheek. "I will always remember and relive the moment you were born. I am so proud of you."

"I've gotta get to school." Tucking his head, Scout felt the flush inch up his face. Maya followed him to the door as did his mom's giggles. "Watch out for her, Maya. You bark at strangers to warn her."

After hugging the dog, Scout locked the door behind him and headed to his car. He pulled out immediately but then sat in the school parking lot. A quick scan of his messages showed both women were anxious to move and were making plans. It was also obvious both thought all plans depended on him. Cramming the phone into his pocket, he entered the school as if he wasn't contemplating stealing an artifact from one of the most famous museums in the world.

Leyna faced the opposite direction and leaned against his locker. Scout threaded his way through the kids to stand inches from her back.

"Project Slithery Swoop is a go."

She jumped then slapped his arm. "Did you really need to scare and mock me at the same time?"

"Sorry." His smile contradicted the word before he leaned down to kiss her. "Good morning."

"It will be now. We should go." Leyna latched onto his hand and pulled him toward the library.

He pulled back and shook his head. "Not yet. I need to handle a few things here then we can talk to Brenley."

"We aren't going straight to the museum to try and find the Snake?" Leyna dropped his hand and avoided his gaze.

"We can't. We need the good doctor's access and information. She has to fly there, but she's making the arrangements now." He scanned the halls, but there were no signs of Brody, Gerard, or Dacey. Scout shook his head again at his twisted paranoia.

"And how are you getting there?"

Looking back to Leyna, Scout felt the weight of the question. It took a few more seconds before he understood the significance of it. He chuckled and tapped a finger against her nose. "First, you were jealous of me dreaming about Dacey. Now, you don't want me flying with Brenley."

"I wasn't jealous then or now. I'm trying to understand the plan, but my partner isn't good at communication." Crossing her arms over her chest, she scowled at him.

Scout backed away when guilt settled like a lead balloon in his stomach. "Sorry, I shouldn't have teased you. This is important. I assumed I'd travel with you. You know I'm clueless about how you Travel. Is it harder to Travel farther distances and longer times? We may need to make multiple trips too."

"I can do it." Her chin angled further up and her gaze narrowed further. "You'll have to provide extra chocolate."

Fight over, she smiled and kissed his cheek. He rolled his eyes but grinned back. Scout couldn't ignore his lies though, at least not all of them.

"Listen, we do need to talk about our plan and a few more things. I've heard something new in my dreams. I've already told Brenley so I'm sure she's checking into it. Did you know the Mayans called tree sap 'blood of trees'? The exhibit contains several pieces made of resin, tree sap. I can see why they wouldn't display that when you have jade and obsidian. My mom prefers diamonds, of course."

She was frowning again, but Leyna also placed a hand over his heart. "Did you get any sleep last night? You've been exhausted lately and you're rambling now."

"That depends on how you define sleep and lately." Winking at her, he leaned against the lockers. "I'm fine, and we have a lot of work to do. I've got to check in with Coach Martin and hand in an assignment on my way. That will buy us a little more time. A lot of seniors start skipping this time of year."

"Want to meet in the library before your second class?"

"Sure, that works. Don't worry – I'll bring some chocolate and we can communicate." He waggled his brows before giving her an exaggerated wink.

She rolled her eyes and walked away. Scout took a minute to appreciate the sight before rushing to his class.

"Mr. Wade, here's my paper. Coach Martin needs to meet with me. Is it okay if I go to his room right now?"

The grey-haired man knocked a stack of papers off his desk when he waved his permission. Scout knelt to pick them up. The religions teacher looked the part of absent-minded professor and rarely seemed to hear their questions or comments. His lectures had become more interesting since he'd branched into world religions.

"Is there a new reading assignment?" Scout waited then turned the top page of the papers to face him. He made a mental note of the book title then nodded to his teacher. Mr. Wade was too busy scribbling on one of the few chalkboards left in their school. "Thank you."

Scout ignored the students and slipped from the room as the bell rang. Coach Martin's class was on the other side of the building. Pausing, Scout eyed the empty hallway. Both artifacts were in the hidden pockets of his cargo pants. He lifted his head and sprinted full speed down the long hall. Sliding through the ninety-degree turn, he ran toward the stairs. The single flight took little time. Scout skidded to a stop but wasn't even winded. He grinned and strolled into his coach's class.

"Good morning, Scout." Coach Martin was sitting on his desk with his feet swinging in small circles. He grinned and offered a piece of paper. "You are all set to volunteer at the museum and will get credit for this special project. Congratulations on that."

"Thank you, sir." Scout folded the paper and slipped it into his backpack. First his mom and now his coach – they were much more impressed by the museum internship than he was. He thought their responses were over the top, but didn't comment. "I am sorry for what happened."

"Are you really?"

"Well, no." Scout smiled when his coach laughed at his honesty. "I am sorry Mr. Richmond blamed you."

Coach Martin shrugged off the concern. "Toby and I

go way back. It's not a problem. I do need you to at least not get caught going forward."

"I'll do what I can to prevent getting caught." Scout smiled for his coach. Getting caught during a museum heist would bring more than a slap on the wrist.

30

Scout nodded to Mrs. Morrison before closing the media room door behind him. "Mrs. Morrison is already watching us."

"She's always watching. I swear she's the real witch." Leyna was perched on the edge of the work table with her tablet in her hands. "Where's my chocolate? I feel I may need it for this discussion."

He handed it over with a half shrug. "I'm sorry I haven't been communicating well. I'd love if we could blame it on lack of sleep."

"Is that the reason?" She toyed with the silver wrapping but didn't open the chocolate.

"No." Telling that single truth didn't hurt. Scout exhaled a harsh laugh. "I struggle to understand the truth of what I see and hear. Even more lately than when I first returned from the Island."

"Why?"

He pulled a chair over but couldn't sit down. Pushing it away, Scout focused on Leyna again. "The FBI agent told me I didn't understand how much power both sides had. He also warned me they would use those closest to me against me."

Leyna hopped off the table and put the chocolate on it. "What do you mean *use people against you?*"

"You were the one who demanded Thomas protect Brenley. Dacey is gone – even the memories of him were erased. Any of you could be taken from me if they want to force me to do something." He kicked the chair and sent it rolling across the room. "I could be the person who ends this world. They could be waiting for me to gather the artifacts to make a move."

"Scout, you aren't responsible—"

"But, I am. That's the only thing everyone agrees on. This wouldn't be happening without me. Take me out of the equation, and it falls apart. They all fail."

Leyna grabbed his shirt and jerked him forward. "No one is taking you out of the equation. We are partners, and I chose to be in this. You didn't have a choice, but I did. So did Brenley. You even said you thought Dacey knew more than he'd shared and he created that painting as a message to you. We all made our choices, and that's not on you."

It was another lie of omission when he nodded. Scout didn't ask Leyna to clarify what choices she had made. He watched her hand release his shirt only to rub over his heart. Placing his hand on hers, he met her eyes again. "It needs to remain an educated decision. Things are changing fast and more things are going to happen. Have you checked out Brenley's notes?"

"She called it the Snake lullaby. Is that how it sounds to you?" She didn't pull away or push closer as she stared up at him.

"That's as good a description as any. The nightmares

are still on the beach more than in the cenote." He tried not to wince at the memories of fire and death. "I think that's my overactive imagination bringing the curse to life."

"The curse Brenley told us about? Are you still worried about that?"

"In the interest of good communication, there's not a lot I'm not worried about right now." He managed a chuckle when she rolled her eyes. "All signs point to the Snake being at the museum, which the rogue agents already know. There's no way we'll be able to waltz in and steal it. I'd rather not add Interpol to the list of people gunning for us."

Leyna laughed then hugged him. "I'm good with the 'us versus them' thing. And you definitely have me on your side. I'm not going anywhere. You know that, right?"

She'd whispered the words against his neck. Scout kept her close. "I know that." He didn't doubt she'd stay. He did doubt why she stayed. "What about finding something normal in this world? Do you still want that?"

"Normal is relative or so I've heard."

Another squeeze then a kiss to her temple and he pulled away. "We need to talk to Brenley and finalize a plan for finding and stealing the Snake. I'd like to review the museum floorplan and..."

"Do your soldier thing." Leyna finished his thought with a grin. "Project Slithery Swoop is a go."

He pressed the button to call Brenley while grinning at Leyna.

"Good afternoon, this is Dr. Golnar."

Grin sliding from his face, it took Scout a second to find his voice. "Are you in trouble?"

"I found another painting." Her tone was polite, professional.

"We're coming to you—"

"No, that won't be necessary. I'm still researching information. Thank you for calling."

"Brenley, do not hang up on me. Tell me where you are." It was surprisingly easy to demand and beg at the same time.

The phone clicked off. Glaring at it, he saw her name and face disappear as the screen went black.

"What's wrong? What did she say? "

"She's in trouble, but she wouldn't tell me where she was." Scout paced in quick circles. He kept the phone in his hand instead of pitching it against the wall.

"How do you know something's wrong?" Leyna reached for him, but he spun to the side and glared at her. "Please talk to me, Scout."

"I told you that I'd put you all in danger. Someone got to her. Brenley was acting – she never uses a greeting like a normal person." Scout pulled back his fist to strike out blindly. A warm iron grip around his wrist stopped him. In the space of a heartbeat, Dacey was there and gone.

"Scout, please." Leyna now had a death grip on his arm.

He blew out a breath and let her pull his arm down. "Let's go to Dacey's house."

"What?" Leyna didn't release his arm, but her grip tightened enough to press her nails into his flesh.

"I have to try. The place should be deserted, right? If she's in trouble because of me…" He couldn't finish the sentence.

"Okay, let's do it." She moved to embrace him then pulled back with a laugh. After she crammed the chocolate into her mouth, she hugged him. "We'll find Brenley."

Scout opened his eyes before his world righted itself. He watched the details snap into focus before his eyes. "I'll never get used to time travel."

Leyna stayed close but turned completely around. "There's no one here."

"Scout?"

He recognized Brenley's voice and ran toward the sound. "Where are you?"

"I told you not to come. How did you know I was here?" The archeologist looked the same – her clothes weren't even wrinkled.

Leyna came to a stop next to Scout. "Are you okay? What happened?"

Brenley looked from Scout to Leyna before sighing. "I was going to update you tonight after I confirmed everything. Our flight isn't until tomorrow evening."

"Our flight?" Scout felt Leyna tense but didn't look at her. "What flight are you talking about?"

"I had a visitor when you called. A blonde boy who looked about your age. He encouraged me to take your call, even though I wouldn't say who was calling."

Scout grimaced and looked away while cursing Gerard in his head. "What did he want?"

Brenley picked up a manila envelope and handed it to Scout. "He congratulated me on joining the task force to study and stop the looting of cultural treasures, trafficking of museum pieces, and rampant forgeries. My part is to study the Mayan exhibit at the Guggenheim."

Leyna's jaw dropped and Scout knew his expression mirrored hers.

"He then asked that I give this to you the next time you visited. He didn't give me a chance to deny anything. He was a rather cocky young man." Brenley's lips pulled back then settled into a flat line once more.

"I can believe that. Did you open it?" Scout held it without making the effort himself.

"He's one of the other agents, isn't he? The ones that support the former leader, Hodges?" Brenley nodded to answer her own questions. "I did look. It's a passport and plane tickets. There's even an ID card listing you as an intern on my research team. He had documentation for me too."

Ripping open the envelope, Scout dumped the contents on the top of a nearby bookshelf. He picked up the plane ticket while Leyna grabbed the passport.

"It looks legit." Leyna waved the passport in Scout's face. "How did they do this? Why did they do it?"

"They have resources like the MMEA. Remember when they came here before? The guy said he wanted to offer me another option. He also said they thought the artifacts belonged to me." Scout studied the ID card granting access to the Guggenheim Bilbao.

"That was a lie to manipulate you. They were ready to kill you once. Have you forgotten that? You can't trust him!" After flinging the passport down, Leyna paced across the room. "It's a trap. It has to be a trap!"

"There was one more thing he said." Brenley's voice sounded quiet after Leyna's outburst.

Scout moved slowly to pick up the passport and avoid looking at the archeologist. He couldn't stop the tension drawing every muscle tight. Gerard was one of the secrets he'd kept from both women. "Don't keep us waiting. What did he say?"

"He said to tell you his name is Gerard and he hopes you two can be friends."

"No, absolutely not!" Leyna screeched the denial and stomped across the room to Scout's side.

"It's okay. I'm not really looking for more friends right now." Scout smiled when Leyna slumped against a chair and took several breaths. He turned to face Brenley. "I guess you and I have a trip to make."

31

Despite Leyna's objections, there had been no time to formulate a better plan, and Scout's parents dropped him off at the airport the next evening.

They'd congratulated him and revealed they'd known for the last week. The grant rules required absolute secrecy to prevent bribes. The fact that he still lived at home required parental permission. Scout had seen the paperwork his parents had received detailing the grant program and his participation. Everything looked official, and his school and the city museum had also enthusiastically supported the trip. He kept his head down, packed, and pretended all was normal.

His parents weren't suspicious. However, Scout viewed it as the threat it was – his enemies could get to his family and friends at any time.

"Are you going to be this tense the entire time?" Brenley leaned close to whisper. Their driver was loading their luggage into the car. The archeologist had been as calm as ever throughout the flights and layovers.

"I thought you were nervous about your first time on a plane."

"Considering my life, a plane crash isn't likely to be the reason I die." Scout grumbled the words but nodded to the driver and smiled for Brenley when he held the car door open for her.

She frowned but slid inside. He joined her in the back without speaking.

"Again, my name is Ander, and I welcome you to our wonderful city of Bilbao. It is my pleasure to be your driver today. We will be on our way in only a minute." Ander smiled at them before closing the door.

Taking advantage of his departure, Scout turned to look at Brenley. "We both know Leyna is partially right. This is a trap. Even if we get the Snake, they're watching us. Setting this up wasn't to help us. It's to control us."

"I know. We've had this discussion several times since yesterday. We all agreed this was our best option. We go along with their plan and try to make it our own. Has anything changed, Scout?"

He glared for a second then rolled his eyes. "No, nothing's changed. This is our only option. I don't want anyone else in danger."

The driver's side door opened and Ander took his seat. He twisted to face them and was again all smiles. "We are on-time and will arrive at the Museo Guggenheim soon. I am to ask if you wish to go to the hotel first. I believe your stay is short, but you have rooms for your convenience. Do you wish for that?"

"Sure." Scout didn't look at Brenley. "It'd be great to stop for a quick minute and change clothes. Thank you very much."

"It is no trouble. We will go there first." Ander started the engine and pulled away from the airport.

Soft music concealed the noise of traffic but didn't dull the roar of blood in Scout's ears. Thoughts and fears had tumbled around his brain constantly since Gerard had visited Brenley. Leyna had updated Thomas and would join them once it was safe. They'd entered the country legally, but Scout was glad to have other options for their departure. A sharp jab to his ribs had Scout returning to the present.

Brenley jerked her head toward the front and scowled at him.

"...you will find many splendid things. Yes, el Museo is beautiful, but Bilbao has ancient stone roots blessed by the salt of the sea. We are also a prized modern city. Only Barcelona..."

Ander's words faded as Scout's mind conjured images of crashing waves along a bloody beach. He reached blindly to roll down the window and pressed closer to breathe fresh air. The cityscape slowly replaced the nightmares, and he became aware of Brenley's hand on his back. After a few more breaths, he could even understand the conversation flowing around him.

"...yes, yes. The wolves are for Don Diego López de Haro, who founded our city." Ander chuckled and tapped one hand against the steering wheel in time with the music. "Not many tourists know our history. I forget that you go to el Museo. I will think of more trivia to best you."

"Good luck with that, Ander." Scout leaned back in his seat with a grin. He pulled the water bottle from his bag and flipped it in his hand. "Dr. Golnar is a very smart woman."

"She knew our flag and our Lee Kuan Yew World City Prize," Ander agreed with another laugh. "We have arrived at your hotel. I will bring your bags around."

They left Ander next to the car as the helpful hotel staff checked them in and rushed them to their rooms. Scout stood in the middle of his without moving. He and Brenley had exchanged key cards, so he didn't flinch when the door opened after a single knock.

"Do I want to know what you're doing?" She'd already changed from her travel clothes and was eating an apple. "You have a fruit basket too."

He knocked the fruit from her hand. "That could be poisoned."

"If we were in a fairy tale, but we're not. You're being paranoid." Brenley picked up the apple and tossed it in the trash.

Scout crossed the room to look out the window again. He was careful to stay to the side. "Just because you're paranoid doesn't mean they aren't out to get you."

"I think you're safe." Brenley met his gaze without flinching. "Remember, you are the only thing everyone agrees on. They even arranged for this trip to happen. They need you to get all four artifacts."

"Or they need to make sure I don't get them and give them to someone else." Scout paced the length of the room.

Brenley brought an apple to him and held another one for herself. "The sugars in apples have a similar effect to caffeine. While I don't need you more tense, I do need you awake and alert."

Juice ran down his chin from the first bite. He wiped it away with his hand and accepted the water she handed him next.

"You need to change your clothes so we can go. Why did you want to stop here if not to freshen up? We aren't planning to stay the night." Brenley stood next to the large painting above the small table.

"It forces them to search a second location instead of knowing all our possessions are with us. They'll see we have options and may even have a different plan." He called out from the bedroom as he changed clothes. After washing his face and brushing his teeth, he rejoined the archeologist to find her in the same place he'd left her. "You okay, Doc?"

"I think I was wrong." Her mouth twitched up at the corners.

Scout grabbed the messenger bag Brenley had given him to use. It was lighter and smaller than his backpack, but still left his arms free. He again verified the Jaguar and Turtle were there before looking up to prompt her to explain.

"You are a warrior." Brenley smiled at him with wide eyes. "I think that is why you're in the middle of this."

"I was a soldier on the Island, but not a warrior. I only did what I was told." He avoided her eyes and tried not to remember the orders he'd followed.

"I've told you about the Mayan warriors. Holcans would have followed orders too. It doesn't mean they weren't fierce warriors." Brenley continued to study him. "I will have to give this more thought. It is not something I factored into my research."

"Sure, whatever. As I am the warrior, do you think you could follow my suggestions for your safety?" Scout approached her with a grin. "We won't have traditional weapons, but anything can be used to defend yourself. If you have the chance to run, you'd better run."

She started to shake her head, but then nodded. "We've already discussed this, and I agreed that we both need to survive this trip."

"I'm guessing that's the best I can get from you. Let's get this show on the road. We have a Snake to find."

Ander greeted them warmly and shared more information as he navigated the streets. Scout was more focused on the city itself. They'd studied maps and uploaded them to their phones as a contingency plan. Seeing the city, even as a blur, helped Scout find his feet and breathe easier. Bilbao was clean and modern, but not dull and grey. Many buildings bore bright artwork on their walls. There were sculptures and fountains dotting the wide streets. He looked ahead and gestured to the red arch.

Brenley leaned over to see then nodded. "La Salve Bridge. We are almost there."

His eyes widened when the shiny whale of a building came into view. Next to the standard square buildings, the waves and circles appeared futuristic, almost alien. "That's the Guggenheim?"

"Yes, of course, it is." Brenley was riffling through her briefcase and didn't even look at the museum. She pulled out their ID cards and authorizations. After placing the lanyard over her head, she handed one to him. It was impossible to miss how her hand trembled. "This is happening too fast. I haven't had time—"

"We've got this, Doc." Scout waited until she looked at him. "I've got your back. Let's do it."

SCOUT STUMBLED AS HE TRIED TO CLIMB THE STAIRS TO THE museum entrance. He froze in place and stared instead of scanning for danger.

Brenley returned to his side and faced the large sculpture. "That's Maman by artist Louise Bourgeois. It is said to represent protectiveness and vulnerability."

"That is a huge-ass spider."

"Yes, she is." Brenley continued forward with her briefcase swinging with each step.

He was forced to jog to reach her. He glanced once more at Maman then followed the archeologist and their guide into the museum.

"One moment. Please wait here, Dr. Golnar."

Studying the pictures hadn't prepared Scout for the experience. White stone, sleek glass, clear windows, and dark metal flowed in an artistic rendering of a building. There was a soft beauty that gave him the feeling of floating through a dream.

"Right this way. You must proceed through security

first, please and thank you." A short, dark-haired man looked only at Brenley to provide instructions.

No longer able to appreciate the beauty of his surroundings, Scout walked next to Brenley. He stood at attention at the security desk until they were waved through. A slow exhale eased the ache in his chest.

The guide stayed by Brenley's side and spoke of the Mayan exhibits. Scout trusted Brenley to pay attention to the eager man. His gaze was on a continuous circuit as they strolled through the public space to reach the private area. When they paused at one display, he pulled out his phone to make notes on the placement of cameras and exits, as well as the number of guards.

They continued back to storage, and Scout stumbled for the second time. It wasn't Maman that demanded his attention. Scout welcomed the humming energy snapping to attention inside him. He could hear the bass beat of his heart as black dots danced on the edge of his vision. Hazy lines further distorted the storage room as it transformed into a dark jungle. It wasn't Chichen Itza or the Island. The hiss of a snake made Scout flinch.

He jerked away from the pull at his side and tried to bring the image back into focus. Another Mayan pyramid stood before him. Dark eyes filled his vision, but no one stood before him. It was again rows of tables and shelves.

"Scout doesn't travel well. Low blood sugar. Do you think you could find us something sweet for him to eat or drink?"

"Yes, of course, Doctor. I will return."

Brenley grabbed Scout's arm. "Are you okay? What happened?"

"It's here." Scout didn't look at her. He started to dig

through his bag when she moved both hands to cover his.

"Hugo will be right back. You can't bring out the artifacts. We need—"

"I need them to find the Snake. I need it!"

The archeologist didn't release his hands, but she frowned at his outburst. "And you will use them to find it. We have authority to review their records on the Mayan exhibit. That is the plan, remember?"

Scout nodded and waited for her to release his hands. He wasn't surprised to see them shake. His heart still raced and his fingertips tingled. "I think that apple had much more of a caffeine impact than coffee."

Brenley snorted, but Hugo returned at the same moment. She took the offering of a cup and a wrapped toffee. "Here you go."

Without speaking, Scout took a drink and tried not to wince at the syrupy liquid. He unwrapped the candy and stuffed it in his mouth.

"Thank you, Hugo. The shaking is certainly a sign of low blood sugar. He might have passed out if you hadn't acted so quickly."

The guide puffed up at her praise. He even managed to nod in Scout's general direction without looking away from the archeologist.

"It is my pleasure to serve you."

"Perhaps we can talk here while my intern recovers. There is much I wish to ask you about your expansion of the exhibit." Brenley pushed Scout onto a stool and leaned against the table next to him.

Scout swallowed more of the drink and ignored their discussion. The feelings were fading, and he needed them back to direct him. He had to grip the cup tightly to avoid reaching for his artifacts again. The Snake was here, and he had to find it. Brenley bumped into him when she moved away. He turned slightly to watch them talk.

"I would love to see the research videos and notes. I understand there were items pulled from storage and combined with our more recent finds."

"Yes, Chichen Itza provided the majority of the pieces, but we included artifacts from Tulum and Ek Balam. We were fortunate to receive a positive response from outside Mexico to truly make the exhibit global."

"I have yet to extend my trips outside the Yucatan. What other locations donated?"

"I am sure you would be welcome at all digs, Dr. Golnar. The governments of Belize and Guatemala loaned us several pieces. We have a lovely figurine from the Lamanai Temple. It is a replica on display currently, so I can show you the original piece if you would like."

"Thank you, Hugo. We would appreciate it. Have you included anything from El Mirador?"

Scout didn't listen to Hugo's response. Another guard stepped through the side door and stopped to stare at them. Adjusting his weight in a wider stance, Scout faced the newcomer. The man was much older than Hugo and twin scars were visible down his throat. He stared back at Scout with one hand resting on the gun strapped to his belt.

A metallic clang echoed through the room. Scout spun around and pulled Brenley away. He scanned for danger but only saw Hugo picking up several tools from the floor.

"My apologies, Dr. Golnar. I fear my exuberance makes me clumsy in your presence." Hugo placed the tools on the work table without looking away from Brenley.

Scout looked to the right again, but the mysterious guard was gone. "That can't be good."

"No, no, it is very good Dr. Golnar is here." Hugo faced Scout for the first time to scowl at him. "She is a friend of Señor Cadmael and she is welcome here."

"Dacey? You know Dacey?" Brenley's professional façade crumbled. Pale and trembling, she swayed on unsteady feet.

Scout stood next to her and placed a hand at her back. She leaned against him for only a second before bolting upright.

"Did Dacey help restore anything for you? Anything recent?"

"Yes, Señor Cadmael helped with the Mayan exhibit, but with others as well. He is a gifted artist. It is my dream to create such beautiful art too, and he was kind enough to offer advice." The guide lowered his head with a small smile.

Brenley slumped against Scout again. She was nodding, but he knew it was in response to her internal monologue and not Hugo's words. Scout wanted to give her a few moments to settle.

"Hugo, my girlfriend loves art. What kind do you do?"

"I work with paint and prefer an abstract style. We need to see the world in color instead of black and white. There is such beauty around us and in us. The human form is far more complex than mere eyes or hands." Hugo twisted his hands together and bit his lip. "I apologize. It is not appropriate to speak of my work to you."

Standing tall again, Brenley smiled at him. "Scout asked the question and we are interested. Perhaps, after we complete our review here, we could see some of Dacey's works and yours as well?"

"I would be honored." Hugo bowed low then beamed at them. "I will leave you to your review. I hope you do find it to be educational, Mr. Ainsley. Studying with Dr. Golnar is an honor indeed."

"Yes, it is," Scout agreed.

"Thank you, Hugo. Please see we are not disturbed." Brenley smiled until the door closed behind the guide. She pivoted to stare at Scout with wide eyes. "Dacey was here."

Scout nodded then held up his hands. "He wasn't the only one though. I saw a guard who didn't look like the others. I think Hodges' men or possibly even Thomas' are here. We need to move fast, but I don't know where to start looking."

"I do." Brenley's lips twisted before settling into a flat, tight line. "I lied to you, Scout."

33

SCOUT STARED AT THE ARCHEOLOGIST. "YOU LIED TO ME."

"Technically, yes." Brenley sat down at the work station and started typing. "However, your lies inspired the strategy."

"Inspired the strategy?" Scout snapped his mouth shut after repeating her words. "This doesn't make any sense. You're the only one without an agenda. You're the only one I trusted. Who got to you?"

She looked up with a smile. "No one...well, technically *you* did. Your trust made this work. At least, I think it will work. We agreed to go along with the plan and look for a way to win. This could be our way to win. Hold on."

Numb, he watched her type and scroll through screens – his usually crowded mind was quiet, blank. Scout wasn't sure how much time passed before she turned back to him.

"I think we have time for you to get the artifacts out now. How will you use them to find the Snake?" Her eyes glowed as she bounced up off the seat. "How did you know the Snake was here?"

"You think I'm going to find the Snake for you?" He stepped away but refused to turn his back on her.

Some of her excitement faded as Brenley studied him. "I haven't explained, have I? This happened faster than I had planned. I wanted to have more evidence before speaking to you. I do not handle change as well as I should." Her body folded forward and swayed again. "It is exhausting to lie. You did not tell that so I wasn't prepared. Then the mention of Dacey confused me too. Studies show a lack of sleep can make one emotional too."

"Catch a wave, Doc, you're drifting." He clenched his fists to keep from offering her comfort when she tilted her head and squinted at him. "Explain your lies."

She took a deep breath and stood tall. "Let me show you something first. I don't need you to find the Snake. I know where it is."

Snarling, he stepped closer but stopped when she didn't back away. "We were supposed to look for information then I was going to call Leyna. She and I would return afterhours to find it. That was the plan."

"Yes, that was the tentative plan, but you don't trust her. I can take you to it, but I thought you'd want to test out the artifacts. You had a vision when we first entered, didn't you? You were adamant about using the Jaguar and the Turtle to find *your* Snake. Do you no longer want to do that?"

Her brow furrowed as if she was confused. Scout almost rolled his eyes at her. "Let's focus on you. How do you know where the Snake is?"

"I found records buried in the files a friend sent me. Scientists often take personal notes and not all use electronic ones. They, whether Thomas or Hodges, couldn't eliminate all such records." Brenley turned the monitor to him. "The location is listed here."

"Why did you lie to me?" The anger seethed deep inside, but there was no overwhelming need to punch the archeologist…yet.

"It was an omission while I gathered the evidence. Then this happened so quickly, so yes, I lied to you. I didn't mean to do that, but I did mean to lie to Leyna. You don't trust her or Thomas. I'm not sure of the exact reason, but a logical guess would be that you think she's working for him."

Scout didn't agree or disagree, but he did mentally curse her intelligence. "What makes you think I don't trust her?"

"I followed the evidence." Her slim shoulders lifted and fell in a small shrug before she lifted a hand with her index finger pointing up. "One – you gave her the job to search for information on Ek Balam and the North Road after you told me you wanted to search for the Snake first, not the Owl. It was that information she then shared with Thomas, who you've stated you do not trust."

She smiled and held up a second finger. "Two – you hadn't told her about your recent dreams or the Snake lullaby. Instead, you called me to talk about these things."

Gritting his teeth, Scout stayed quiet and glared at her.

"Three came more from Gerard. He provided information to me and arranged for you and me to work together. If Leyna was on his team or neutral like me, he would have included her."

Scout's mouth fell open at her words. "I didn't think about it like that."

"Leyna does work for Thomas then?" Brenley asked as she lowered her hand.

"Yes, but others told me. She has never mentioned it." After scrubbing a hand over his face, he shook his head. Instead of the usual rush of energy, he felt drained. "This doesn't matter right now. Let's get back to the Snake."

"Do you want to try and find it or have me tell you where it is?" Brenley's voice was as calm as ever.

Scout scowled at her. "I feel like you're challenging me because you don't believe I can find it."

She actually laughed and placed a hand on his shoulder. "I am curious, I'll admit to that. I also like you. You're weird like me, like Dacey. It is a strange connection I do not understand. Aren't you curious about what you can do as the Guardian of these artifacts? If they have power and you have power, perhaps you can get Dacey back to us. Am I rambling again? I've never felt like this before. It is very bizarre."

He didn't answer, but he did turn away from her. Now, his thoughts raced in circles. She had figured out so much on her own, but she didn't know about Dacey. Scout wasn't sure what he knew about the man either. His thoughts sputtered to a stop – Leyna.

"There is a way to test my theory that you don't trust Leyna. If I'm wrong, I will apologize to you both." Brenley waited until Scout faced her again. "Call her and tell her what I've done."

Scout held Brenley's gaze, pulled out his phone, and put it on speaker. Leyna answered before the first ring was complete. "Hey, we're in the museum. I think Hodges' guys are here too. Brenley has a theory about personal records from the scientists providing help. We're going to look into that."

"Great, I can—"

"No, that's okay. There's something else we need you to check. The guide mentioned knowing Dacey. I know we haven't found information on Dacey, but you can check out a museum employee named Hugo. Said he wants to be an artist too."

"I can do that. Are you sure you don't need me there?"

"No, we'll stick to the plan and search first. Call if you find something and we'll do the same."

Scout finished the call and clicked it off. "I don't trust her completely, but now I don't trust you either. She'll at least have some information to go by if this all goes south."

Her eyebrows drew together again when she frowned. "I think my theories and strategy are solid. Even if you can't find the Snake, I have its location. I'll write it down."

"That's not what I meant." Scout rolled his eyes as she wrote down something on a scrap of paper. "I meant that if you're screwing me over, Leyna might be able to stop whatever real plan you have.'

"I told you my real plan. I have always tried to help you."

Memories of their conversations flashed in Scout's mind. His instincts screamed to trust her, but he didn't want to make another mistake with lives on the line. He tried to compile the evidence as she had. "You asked me about lying and how I handled everything. I thought it was strange that you argued with Leyna about being here." He stopped before admitting he believed her.

The archeologist stood quietly before him – calm and stoic as always. Her face remained pale though and her hands were clutched together.

"You love Dacey. You want answers for the sake of

knowledge, not power." The connection he'd always felt with her remained strong.

"Yes."

He scrubbed a hand over his face and nodded. "Then tell me the rest of your plan. Tell me what you've discovered about the Snake." Scout kept a hand on his bag and his back against a table. There were exits on both sides and metal tools that could easily become weapons. He couldn't bring himself to think he'd need protection from Brenley.

"The researchers' notes included a resin snake with white and red markings. Though not as striking as obsidian or jade, it fits the style and time and is an excellent example of Maya culture. It was marked to be included in the exhibit. I found a listing of a snake in the restoration department here. It was listed with the Maya pieces, but isn't linked to the inventory. I'm not sure if that omission was intentional or not, but it kept others from finding it. I found it because I knew exactly what to look for and where. Since its initial evaluation, it had been damaged. There's a small chip along the middle left side." Brenley turned her tablet to him and showed him handwritten notes.

"So while everyone is trying to find the Snake in the displays, you knew it was safely tucked away in the restoration department. Once we got here, you also knew it would be easy to find the piece. That is a clever plan." He wasn't sure whether to be impressed or annoyed.

The archeologist seemed to understand his indecision. "I did lie to you, but I have also tried to help you. I carried on your attempts to mislead the others. Whether they searched based on Chichen Itza or Ek Balam, I was counting on them not knowing about the Snake kings associated with Guatemala." Brenley tapped the pen against her leg in a lazy rhythm.

Something sparked a memory, but it took Scout a second to place it. "That is what you were asking Hugo about earlier."

"Yes, in case he is questioned, the conversation will probably bore most people. You weren't paying attention and you were right beside me." She gave him a pointed look and lifted her chin.

"So, Snake kings in Guatemala?" Scout tried to keep the conversation going as his palms started to itch. He wanted to use the artifacts; he wanted to find the Snake.

"Do you remember when I said Mayas weren't like the Incans? I told you power was divided among families. Once we determined the original Guardian failed, it made sense to me that the strongest families may have been able to claim the artifacts. Having extra abilities during war would interest any Mayan ruler."

"You're brilliant." Scout couldn't help but smile when Brenley grinned. He also couldn't help but shudder dramatically. "You're also a little terrifying."

"Scout." Brenley injected a great deal of annoyance into his name.

"It's true. It's also true that I still trust you. I may regret it—"

"You won't."

He ignored her interruption. "But, I still trust you. Let's test the artifacts and find the Snake."

Scout removed the Jaguar and the Turtle and placed them on the table. Brenley stayed several feet away, but her eyes were bright and curious. He smiled and turned his back on her to close his eyes. Bringing an image of Maya to mind, he pictured the dog in detail. Breathing slow and easy, he opened his eyes and picked up both artifacts. They returned him to the unfamiliar Mayan jungle. Wisps of white clouds floated on the edges of his vision. His breathing became shallow, but the heat pulsing through his body felt safe.

Images floated through his mind. Snakes – an older man – a child – crashing ocean waves – alien jungle chirps and howls.

The blue jade owl and the patient white snake,
Hunt together during the night,
Prey for prey,
The circles of life rarely ever break,
Destiny is your own to create

It became harder to breathe as the clouds became heavier and darker. A smoky, spicy taste made him swallow hard.

Scout's stomach plummeted as his head cleared. He was still in the museum, but the room looked very different.

"You walked straight here." Brenley's face was pale and wide-eyed. She held up the scrap of paper then pointed to a number on a file cabinet and read the label. "2014 – BF25."

Scout glanced at the cabinet then the number on the piece of paper. Both read 2014 – BF25.

34

His hands trembled as he opened drawer 2014 – BF25. The Jaguar and the Turtle sat on top of the cabinet inches from his face. Flashes of heat and cold rocked his body, but Scout couldn't stop. He looked down at the felt-lined drawer divided into several smaller sections. The silver dagger and thin white cylinder held no appeal to him. His gaze locked on the coiled Snake. He placed one hand on it and lifted it out.

Blinding flashes of orange and red brought pinpricks of pain behind his eyes. Scout could smell the mixture of damp earth, pine, and blood. The forest surrounded him once more. Fire spiraled through his body, leaving goose-bumps and trembling muscles behind. The rush of water was softer than crashing waves and birds chirped in the distance. A second later, the scene disappeared.

When he turned to Brenley, he saw tear tracks down her face and the redness of her eyes. "Are you okay?" he asked.

"Am I okay?" She swiped the tears away and forced

air through her nose. Muscles flexed along her jawline as she gritted her teeth.

Scout placed the Snake next to the Jaguar and the Turtle. He paused for a second as a feeling of joy swept through him. Laughter pushed up, but he cleared his throat and turned back to the archeologist. "Are you going to tell me why you're crying?"

She glared at him for several seconds. "I was concerned when you froze in place for seven and a half minutes. Your eyes were closed, and you were barely breathing. You were deathly pale. If you'd been anyone else, I would have called for help."

"Seven minutes? That can't be right. It was only a second." Scout pivoted back to hold the Snake again. He looked back to find Brenley staring blankly at him.

"You must learn to control the speed of the Snake. There is no time now." Dacey stood next to the archeologist. "They are coming for you. Do not be afraid to use your power, but take care."

"It was seven and a half minutes." Brenley almost yelled at him.

He and Brenley were alone in the room. Scout took a slow breath and counted the seconds of his exhale.

"Scout? You're going to have to put that thing down. We can't afford to have you incapacitated. You are the only person I trust, and we're getting out of here together." Brenley reached for him then pulled back and clenched her fists. She stared at the artifact as if it were a real snake preparing to bite her.

"Okay, I'll put them all away. We need to get back…to wherever we were. Can you get us there? I don't remember walking here." Scout didn't wait for a reply. He wrapped all three artifacts up and stashed them in his bag.

Brenley was several feet away when he turned back. She gestured for him to follow.

"Remind me of this next time so I don't want to test out any other theories."

There was a childish pout in her tone that made Scout laugh. "Do you believe in the magic of the artifacts now?"

"They are not magic," Brenley immediately contradicted. She stopped and faced him, but she was staring at his bag. "I've been thinking about that too. Science in its current form cannot explain this. Factoring in time travel, it's certainly possible that future technology has advanced sufficiently for this all to be possible, even normal."

He couldn't stop the laughter now. "I was hoping for space cowboys myself."

The exasperated sigh was Brenley's version of rolling her eyes. She didn't bother to respond before leading him back to the workstation. It was the first time he noticed the trays of artifacts that were clearly Mayan in origin. There were also stacks of files and flash drives.

"What is all of this?"

"You truly didn't listen at all, did you?" Brenley gestured to the tables surrounding them. "Remember the lie? We are part of a grant team researching museum practices to combat thefts and forgeries. I will need to file some type of report."

He sat down as she scanned the boxes. There was no longer a desire to laugh, but he was considering the possibility of a nap when his phone buzzed. "It's Leyna."

"What are you going to tell her?"

Scout stared at Leyna's image while the phone continued to buzz. "Nothing yet. I'll call her back in a few minutes. What do you think we should say?"

"Are we a 'we' again? Do you still trust me?" The lines of her thin face softened as she sat next to him. "This happened very fast, and it was my first attempt at subterfuge."

"You fooled me and all of us, so I'd say you were a natural." Scout winked at her.

"I find I do not like it. I have not slept well and even I have nightmares. It is exhausting to lie. How do people do it all the time? How do you do it?" Her head dropped forward as she rubbed small circles against both temples.

Memories of their late-night discussions made Scout smile. "Maybe we should both add alcohol to our coping mechanisms."

He rolled his eyes and nudged her side when she sighed. "Deflection, Doc. You have to learn the art of trash talk. Don't worry. I can teach you. We can add it to our late night chats when we get back home."

"I enjoyed our talks even though I didn't share all of my thoughts. I had planned to talk to you, but this happened very fast. I had to make a choice with the evidence I had." Brenley folded her hands in her lap and looked down.

"I'm sorry, Doc. We bombarded you with everything all at once. I don't know that I've made the best choices so I can't condemn you."

"But can you trust me?" It took a couple of seconds for her to look him in the eyes.

"Yes. I've trusted you from the beginning. It was a connection I felt but couldn't explain. There's not a whole lot that I can explain. I try to keep the good things close and even my therapist says I need friends." He watched some of the pain ease from her face. "I'll be honest with you. There are things I've kept from you too. I'm doing it to protect you, and I'll keep doing that."

"You're a warrior." Brenley stood and stretched before moving back to the trays. "We have work to do. This will go faster if I check the pieces and you type my notes. We'll have something to submit as a preliminary report before we leave."

Scout moved toward the computer, but Brenley stopped him with a hand on his shoulder.

"You need to call Leyna. Tell her we found it, but we're sticking to the cover story for our protection. I don't think she'll send Thomas' agents rushing in to take it."

"No, she won't. They still need us to find the Owl." He slid past the archeologist and sat down. Flexing his fingers out from clenched fists, he picked up his phone.

Leyna again answered quickly. "Are you okay?"

"Yeah, sorry about that. The guide was with us and I didn't want to talk in front of him."

"What's going on?"

Scout met Brenley's gaze and smirked. "You won't believe this, but we have the Snake." He held the phone back at her exclamation.

"Yes, we have it. We're going to complete the cover story so they don't get suspicious. We'd also like to see Dacey's art. Did you find anything about Hugo?"

There was silence then brief tapping. "I found an employee with that name who does have art all over his social media sites. Looks abstract and entirely too bright to me. He's in art school. Do you need all of this?"

"As long as you think he's legit, it's good enough for me. Anything in there concern you?" Scout looked down and forced his hands off the strap of his bag. He glanced back and found Brenley sorting through artifacts.

"No, there's nothing that jumps out at me. When should I get there?"

Scout didn't bother to say they didn't need her since they'd located the Snake. "We need time to finish the cover story and see the art. I'll text when we have the room to ourselves and you can hop over and check out the Snake."

"Okay, I think it's smart to stick with the cover. If Hodges has men there, they may decide not to let you leave."

"That's why you're joining us. I haven't seen Brenley in a fight, but I know you."

Leyna laughed. "Good to have my skills appreciated, soldier boy."

"Oh yeah, I appreciate your skills." Scout smiled as her laughter stuttered then bubbled up again.

"Scout, you should focus on the work." Brenley's tone was sharp, but her lips twitched up at the corners.

"Sorry, Leyna. Brenley is a tough boss and I have to work. We'll call you later."

Brenley stared at him for several seconds. "I'll have to steal your words. You are terrifying."

He blinked then realized what she meant. "Well, I've been lying since Atlantic Island. It doesn't get easier, but you do get better at it."

"I don't think I want to get better." The archeologist cleared her throat then started sharing her notes.

The work proved to be a nice distraction from his worries about Leyna, Brenley, and the new artifact in his bag. Scout's neck and shoulders ached when they wrapped it up hours later.

35

Hugo had left them alone in the small café with an array of food. Scout wolfed his down and stole pieces of Brenley's fruit salad. Her bites were interspersed with long moments of staring into space. Slurping down the last of his soda, Scout leaned forward to rest his elbows on the table. "What's up, Doc?"

She frowned at the question. "Nothing. I am simply considering our current predicament."

"Thinking about 'what if' will drive you crazy. Trust me, I know." Giving her a lazy smile, he continued to watch her. She was pale and her mouth remained a thin line as she picked at her food.

"Do you think Dacey left you a message here? We didn't ask when Hugo last saw him. If Dacey mentioned me, there might be something we are supposed to find." Her hands moved from the food to the napkin. She folded it into a precise square.

"I think Dacey expected problems, and he wanted to help us. I don't think he would've wanted you in danger. You two seem close."

Humor flashed briefly in her eyes before she looked back to the napkin. Her hands smoothed it out then started folding again. "I still feel like my memories, my time was stolen. Without you, I think I would have lost him completely. I might have realized what I'd had."

Scout swallowed hard and bit back the words that blamed him for her loss. It wouldn't ease her pain any more than the information he continued to withhold. He did place a hand on Brenley's to keep her from refolding the napkin. "Would it be lame to say he's the one who lost something valuable?"

She smiled and slipped one hand free to place it over his. "Yes, it would be lame, but I appreciate it."

He leaned back and scanned the area once more. "Wanna find Hugo and see what Dacey was up to then?"

Before they could clean up the mess, Hugo was by their table taking over the task.

"Do you have time to show us Dacey's art and your own?"

Scout wasn't surprised that Hugo almost tripped over his feet trying to discard the trash while looking at Brenley.

"Yes, yes. I can show you these things. Please, come with me. This way."

Waving Brenley forward, Scout brought up the end. He couldn't afford to get distracted by the building while looking for suspicious people. The crowds had thinned with the end of the day approaching. There were still too many for Scout's comfort. He was glad when Hugo led them to a small room in the back.

"Señor Cadmael worked on both restoration and souvenirs for el Museo. This piece is the most recent replica. It is from El Mirador."

Scout was certain he stopped breathing when Hugo

removed the covering to reveal the large canvas piece that looked like their parchment scroll.

"The theory is that the ruling families were represented here. The current research teams feel it is a symbol of the Snake kings." Hugo stepped aside and folded his hands in front of his body.

Giving Brenley a push forward, Scout followed. Neither of them touched the replica, but they continued to stare at it. The four animals were in their familiar compass positions.

"Do you believe it is a crest of some kind? What are these lines?" Her hand trembled as it hovered in mid-air above the lines.

"I will tell them your thoughts on a crest. The families could have unified briefly. What if—"

"I am only guessing, Hugo. The meaning of the piece would be connected to its location and surrounding pieces. Are you aware of those details?" Brenley's tone was calm despite the tremor in her hands.

Hugo gave a series of short bows. "Yes, of course. I can find this out for you. I do not believe we have any pieces. This image was discovered in a cenote and was shared as a courtesy through Señor Cadmael's connections."

"I understand. Thank you. Are there more pieces?" Brenley hadn't looked away from the large painting.

"If you are ready, yes, there is more to see." Hugo backed toward the door and waited.

Scout tugged Brenley away when she made no effort to move. "Doc, let's go."

"Is this the finished version?" She finally turned to face Hugo.

"Yes, it is. It is to be part of the final night of the exhibit. El Museo has planned to include the Mayan pieces as part of a special event. I can request your name be added to the guest list if you'd like."

"Thank you. I would appreciate that." Brenley glanced at the art once more before following the guide.

Scout joined them in the hallway and noted the older guard had returned. He wasn't alone this time. The mountain of a man next to him didn't even wear a uniform. He did have a gun holster though. "Brenley."

She stopped and turned back to him and Hugo did as well. Scout didn't look away from the two men marching toward them.

"They are only guards though they do not usually patrol this area. I'm sure it's nothing to be worried about, Dr. Golnar."

"I'm equally sure it *is* something to worry about. We need to get out of here." Scout tossed his phone to Brenley. "Call Leyna and give her our location."

"I do not understand your worries. I will show them my security credentials."

The men were almost upon them. Scout tried to pull Hugo back, but the man shoved him back.

"I will handle this for Dr. Golnar."

Scout was moving on to Plan B. "There's an exit up there. We need to get back to the public area."

"What about Hugo?" Brenley clutched the phone.

The guide fell to the ground after a single punch. Scar and Mountain marched forward.

"Run, Brenley." Scout turned his back to her as the men charged.

Scar reached him first – Scout slid forward and pivoted to trip him. An extra push sent him careening to the ground. Mountain's wild roundhouse was easy to avoid; the uppercut that followed wasn't. Scout saw stars and stumbled back. Scar wrapped his arms around Scout from behind.

Jamming his elbows back, Scout heard the larger man grunt at the strike. His grip loosened enough for Scout to twist to the side. He slammed the back of his hand into the man's face. The bone cracked with a sickeningly familiar crunch. Blood spurted from the man's broken nose.

A body shot landed with a thud against Scout's ribs. He wasn't fast enough to protect himself. The second punch was a kidney shot. Pain reverberated through his body.

"Hey, why don't you pick on someone your own size?"

Leyna stood a few feet away with her hands on her hips. Brenley was visible behind her.

"I knew this wasn't going to be easy." Scout used the Mountain's distraction to make his move.

A kick to the back of the knees dropped the man to the ground. Scout imagined he could feel the earth shake under them at his fall. The man twisted to look back. His face still reached Scout's shoulders. It was the perfect height for a side kick. His blood gushed faster than Scar's had. Scout's boot had connected with Mountain's mouth and nose to snap his head back. He landed with a thud on the tile floor.

Pivoting, Scout blocked Scar's grab. He didn't give the man a second chance to attack. Low kick – right block – palm strike. Leyna slipped up behind Scar and pointed the small box in her hands at him. Sparks flew before Scar convulsed and fell to the ground. She turned and applied the taser-like weapon against Mountain before he could regain his feet.

"What is that?"

"A gift from Thomas. I can send these thugs to his headquarters if you're okay with that." Leyna opened her jacket to reveal a black vest. Metal glinted from various places. She pulled out another small box.

"Sure, go for it. I don't even want to know what else you have there." Scout walked past them to Brenley. "Do we need to talk about what it means to run?"

"You're covered in blood." She was pale but glaring.

"But, I'm not dead so it's all good."

36

Scout wiped the blood from his hands and face, but he couldn't do much about his shirt. He returned to the hall where Leyna and Brenley were waiting. "Thanks for handling those guys."

"You were the one who fought them. I only cleaned up." Leyna grinned then hugged him. "Good job, soldier boy."

"It was Scar I saw first. Mountain was an unexpected and unwelcome surprise." Scout turned to Brenley. "You okay, Doc?"

"Mountain?" Brenley had her arms wrapped around her chest and was still pale.

Scout moved to her side and rubbed his hands up and down her arms. "People rarely introduce themselves before they attack. I'll try to get real names next time."

"Next time?" It was more of a croak before Brenley started laughing hysterically.

"I think she's in shock." Leyna reached into another vest pocket. "Here, Doc. I'll share my chocolate. It really does make anything better."

Brenley pulled back and struggled to breathe through the mix of laughter and tears. "Thanks."

"She never shares with me so you must be in bad shape." Scout didn't even flinch when Leyna elbowed his ribs for the comment. He did step away to give Brenley space to breathe. Believing him to be a warrior and seeing blood from a battle were two very different things. "Come on, Doc. We've got this. We need to try to leave through the front door to avoid suspicions."

"What about Hugo?"

"He's breathing, but I shocked him too." Leyna shrugged and rolled her eyes. "You want him waking up right now? I don't. He shouldn't remember anything."

"The security feed will probably remind him unless they took care of that." Scout glanced up at the two closest cameras.

"They did, but Thomas added another layer of protection for us. He's helping us as much as you'll allow, Scout." Leyna tugged on her earring and gestured to Hugo's body. "Thomas will make sure he's okay. He really does try to protect people, especially the innocent ones."

"With the cameras done, at least we can get back to the workstation. We'll need to make sure everyone sees us leaving and we should report Hugo's absence. You ready to move, Brenley?" Scout continued to watch the hall, but there were no new threats.

"Yes, I am." Brenley reached out for Scout's hand. "Thank you for protecting me. I know you tried to protect Hugo too. That's what warriors do."

Scout knew his face was pink and avoided looking at either woman. "We aren't out of danger yet. Let's get a move on so we can make that red-eye flight out of here."

He led the way back down with Brenley behind him

and Leyna following. Scout moved them slowly through the building as he tried to avoid people. It was easier to breathe when they were alone in the workroom.

"Can I see it?" Leyna stood by his side bouncing on her toes.

Scout didn't answer, but he did exchange a quick look with Brenley. He pulled out all three artifacts still wrapped in fabric. Careful not to touch the Snake, he arranged them for Leyna's inspection.

She reached out, paused, and then picked up the Snake. After only a second, her shoulders slumped. "I don't feel anything from this one either. What happened when you touched it?"

Brenley's laugh was harsh and short.

Scout sent her a look then grinned at Leyna. "You're both jealous, that's all. The artifacts like me better than you."

"Something did happen then? Do you have some inhuman speed now?" Leyna placed the Snake down before touching the other artifacts. "I really feel nothing."

Instead of wrapping them up, Scout picked up the Jaguar and the Turtle. Warmth curled up to wrap around him like a comfortable blanket. The aches from the fight immediately eased as a cool breeze wafted over him. The scent of pine filled his nostrils. Adjusting his grip, he held both pieces in one hand. He stared at the Snake and imagined it stared back at him.

"Scout?" Leyna's voice sounded far away.

He didn't look away from the Snake, even when he heard Brenley's whisper.

"Please be careful."

When he opened his eyes, the Snake was in his hand and he stood in a jungle once again. The scents of pine and earth filled his nostrils before a sharper metallic smell invaded the moment. Blood. It was an odor Scout recognized.

He lifted his head to look away from the Snake. There was no pyramid this time. It was a dark cenote that waited before him.

Xibalba…Xibalba…Xibalba

The voices called to him before he heard someone, something scream. He turned slowly and found himself facing a line of four warriors. There was no time to differentiate among their body paint and headdresses. One thrust a spear between his ribs.

"Scout, are you going to pick up the Snake?"

He looked down, but there was no blood. There was no wound and no warriors. The Snake still sat on the table. Only the Jaguar and the Turtle were in his hands. "How long?"

"Twenty-two seconds."

Scout nodded at Brenley's answer and put the arti-facts down before he dropped them. His whole body spasmed with enough force to snap his teeth together.

"Scout!"

He wasn't sure who screamed, but both women reached for him. Scout twisted away and raced forward as a man burst through the door.

The short battle was a hazy blur of pain and blood. Blinking, Scout stared at the man. Scout had his hands locked around the stranger's throat. He couldn't waste time wondering how he'd gotten there. The man's dark eyes showed no fear. Scout's fist smashed the man's smirk.

"Move."

Scout's body obeyed the order before his mind understood it. He rolled to the side and stood. Dacey stood over the man who was frozen in place. The silver cylinder in his hand glistened in the light.

"I don't know what it's called, but it has the power to move you through time and space. He only wanted to distract you. I told you to use the power wisely."

Time caught up with Scout in the space of a heartbeat. Dacey was gone and Leyna was charging forward. She kicked the man's weapon away and slammed something against his chest. Scout's attacker disappeared – only splatters of blood remained.

Another spasm shook Scout's body hard enough to drop him to his knees. He pushed Leyna away and stood on shaky legs. Fire pulsed through his body with each beat of his heart. His vision was colored by orange and red hues.

He didn't pick up the silver object, but he blocked it from Leyna. "This is like your weapon. It forces people to Travel."

Leyna flinched then nodded. "Yes, it's an MMEA weapon. Hodges' men would have them too."

"And you have one because you're MMEA." Scout didn't ask, he growled the accusation.

She glanced wildly around the room before looking at him again. Tears welled in her eyes. "I've been trying to tell you. I did lie to you at the beginning, but only about why I was there."

"Thomas needed someone to keep an eye on me. I was a danger to him. I still am."

"No!" She stepped toward him then stopped. "He felt guilty that his choice to save Atlantic Island left you hurting. He was worried about what would happen to you. After he told me about you, I was worried too. You know my history. I felt I understood you."

"You understand nothing." Scout walked toward the

artifacts without looking at her again. Brenley didn't move or comment when she held his bag out to him. He wrapped all three up and placed them inside the bag. "You can tell Thomas that I don't trust him, and he's not getting the artifacts."

"Scout, please let me explain. I know I hurt you—"

"Not really. I've known about your job for a while now." He smirked at her then winked. "It's been fun having you around, but I didn't trust you. You sure as hell don't have the power to hurt me, witch."

The slap made a resounding noise but didn't even turn his face. He smiled and waited to see if she would use her skills to try and inflict real damage.

She brushed the tears away and glared at him. "You aren't blameless in this. I've made mistakes. You have too. I know you've been lying to me and using me against Thomas."

"I don't deny lying to you. Was I supposed to let you manipulate me?"

"You were supposed to talk to me, to let me talk to you." Her voice faltered, but she swallowed hard and lifted her head. "Whatever brought us together, I thought we found something special. Just us, me and you. We became partners and I've never had that with anyone else."

He stood still and watched her.

"The only lie I told was why I was there. The rest was the truth. Can you say the same, Scout?"

The colors receded from his vision, but a cold, hard pressure wrapped around his heart and lungs. He didn't need to see the ocean waves to feel like he was drowning.

Without another word, Leyna disappeared.

37

Scout let Brenley handle their departure. He forced himself to stay alert, even in the public areas of the museum. It wasn't easy since it felt like he was slogging through swamp mud. Each step required more energy than it should; it required more energy than he had.

Slouching in the back seat of their car, he ignored the pleasantries Brenley exchanged with their new driver. The window felt cool against his forehead as he watched the world outside blur by. He was grateful to see each road sign with an airplane. The numbers listed continued to get smaller. When he saw the large sign, he let his eyelids fall and stay closed.

"Scout, we're here. We need to check in and get food." Brenley pushed and prodded him through the appropriate lines and actions until they reached their gate.

"You stay here. There's food right there and I'm going to get us something. You will eat whatever I bring you."

She returned before Scout could formulate a reply.

"Sandwich and chips. Water." She handed him each item from the bag. "Eat and drink, Then we'll talk."

He ate but they didn't talk. Scout felt his body shaking and flung an arm up to defend himself.

"Scout, it's me. Brenley."

Blinking didn't clear his vision. Scout rubbed his eyes and tried again. The archeologist's face slowly came into focus. "Doc?"

"Yes, wake up. We are boarding soon." She continued to shake him until he grumbled and stood.

"I've submitted our report and texted your parents for you. I doubt you'll remember this conversation as you haven't remembered the others. I had to assure two people you weren't drunk. They probably believe I've drugged you."

He chuckled at the words and she stood to frown at him. She even pinched his side.

"Are you with me now, really?"

"Yes, I'm awake and right here." Scout rolled his shoulders and head before stretching up and twisting. His back and neck popped but it didn't hurt. Nothing in his body hurt until the flashes of memories returned.

"There was another guy, just one, right?"

"What did you see before you attacked him?" Brenley leaned close to whisper her question.

"I attacked him?" Scout could see warriors in face paint, but the final man he'd fought was faceless.

Brenley looked around them then nodded. "Yes, you headed toward the door before he came through. Don't get me wrong. I'm glad you went on the offensive, but I don't know how you knew to do that. You hadn't touched the Snake."

"Yes, I had. At least, I remember touching it. I saw a jungle then I saw warriors."

The boarding announcement interrupted them.

"We are not finished with this. Go." Brenley handed him his ticket and passport before tugging him behind her.

After they were in the air, she released her seat belt and twisted to face him. "We have to figure out what happened."

"What did it look like to you?"

"Like you snapped and became an entirely different person." She winced and blew out a harsh breath. "I'm sorry. Now is probably not the best time for bluntness, but I was…"

"Scared?" Scout patted her hand and focused on her. The images and noises in his head were growing louder, but he needed to take this moment with Brenley. "There's nothing wrong with being scared."

"I think terrified might be a better description." She clung to his hand.

"Regardless, you got us out of the museum and all the way here. You took care of me and I owe you for that." He squeezed her hand then softened his grip. "Thank you."

She released his hand and relaxed back into her seat. "I'm glad you're back."

"Yeah, me too." Scout almost laughed at telling her another lie; he wasn't entirely sure who he was anymore. The nightmares had become his reality and he wasn't sure he was ready or able to face them.

Brenley nudged his shoulder. "I am glad you're back, but you aren't getting out of talking about this. I changed my flight so I'll be going to Virginia too. You mentioned changing my routine so I thought it might be a smart strategy."

"It can't hurt to change things up. Plus, you'll get to

meet my parents now. You do realize you'll have to lie to them too, right?" He couldn't resist teasing her.

Face blank, she held his gaze. "I would like to take notes while you talk – handwritten, nothing electronic."

She was pulling out paper and a pen before he even agreed. Turning to him, she held the pen and nodded.

"This feels like therapy. Just so you know, Dr. Wake gives me candy after my sessions."

"I'm sure I can find something. Let's get started." Brenley tapped her pen against the notepad then frowned. "Do you want to talk about Leyna first?"

"No, I don't think now is the time to spill my guts about her. There's really not much to share anyway. Brenley?" Scout paused when he noticed all color had drained from her face.

"I would prefer you didn't spill your guts." The words were stilted, her tone harsh.

"Sorry, Doc. Probably a little too early for those jokes." Scout winced and avoided her gaze.

"Definitely too early. Just tell me what you remember about the Snake." The pen trembled in her hand, but her words were soft and calm.

"Okay. The images in my head, the nightmares, are getting stronger. It's like I'm actually in a different place."

"Or a different time." Brenley stopped writing and tapped her pen. "Something isn't right. You blanked out for seven and a half minutes when you first touched it, but only twenty-two seconds the next time. What did it feel like to you?"

"The first time felt like mere seconds. The next time… it felt like at least a minute. Both times felt like I was somewhere else." The sights and scents bubbled up and left Scout's stomach churning. His muscles bunched and trembled with the need to move, to fight. He swallowed more water and tried to breathe calmly.

When the archeologist hummed and nodded like a real therapist, Scout smiled. The memories were still there, but his body wasn't trying to fight to survive. "The second time when I thought I'd picked it up, I saw four warriors."

"Can you describe them?" Brenley scribbled without looking up.

"Face paint and headdresses, but each one was different. I didn't have long to look before one stabbed me with a spear in the ribs." Anger pulsed softly, but Scout was able to resist the impulse to hit or run. "When I turned around, it's like I knew the warrior was there and was going to stab me."

"That fight was so fast. The other times it almost looked slow by comparison. I know the human fight or flight response alters our perception. Eyewitnesses are normally bad under the best circumstances. I don't think I could pick any of those guys out of a lineup."

"Seriously? You can't remember the difference between Scar and Mountain?" Scout smiled when the woman laughed as she continued to write. He was almost feeling like his version of normal. "Normal is definitely relative."

Brenley looked up, but he waved off her concern and offered an explanation. "I was just thinking that I feel normal, but then I realized that I'm..."

"Not normal." Brenley smiled and nodded. "Yes, I'm starting to appreciate that word differently now myself. Let's get back on subject."

"I don't remember the second fight. I only remember looking down at him and ramming my fist into his face."

"And then what?" Brenley tapped the pen and studied him.

"And then I heard the order to move so I did. I didn't know why but I moved. Dacey was the one who had warned me. He told me the weapon could have allowed them to capture me. He warned me to use the power wisely."

"Dacey was there? Like the dream?"

"I don't know how to explain it. I think—" Scout snapped his mouth shut when the flight attendants delivered snacks.

More people moved around the cabin. By silent agreement, he and Brenley put off the rest of their discussion. The stale crackers and soda provided little distraction. Scout's mind continued to replay images of the warriors and Dacey. The man he'd fought remained a mystery. He couldn't wait any longer and turned to ask Brenley questions. She was sound asleep. After wrapping his blanket around her, he was left to his thoughts.

Blood – warriors – death – darkness.

Knowing sleep wouldn't help, Scout stayed awake during the remaining flights. Brenley was lethargic and grumpy, but he felt rested and alert. He guided her through the last legs of their journey as she had done for him at the beginning.

38

"Come on, Doc. We are finally home. You need to get some sleep and then we'll continue my therapy session." He breathed a little easier when she smiled.

"You shouldn't have let me sleep so long. There's still work to be done. Don't you think—"

"There's always work to be done. We have three of the four artifacts and we're alive. Personally, I think we should celebrate." He saw his parents standing in the distance. "For now, we need to play nice with my parents. Smile and lie, Doc."

He strode forward and almost laughed as Brenley dragged herself slowly behind him.

"Welcome back, son." His mother hugged him as if he'd been gone for weeks.

"Thanks. It's good to be home." He pulled away and smiled at her. "How's Maya?"

"Your little dog is fine." His mom patted his cheek then straightened his shirt.

"It's good you were able to experience business travel. It's not as glamorous as everyone believes. Did you see anything more than the airport and museum?" His dad chuckled and clapped a hand on his shoulder.

"That was about it – definitely not glamorous." Scout grinned as Brenley finally joined them. "I'd like to introduce you to Dr. Brenley Golnar."

"It's nice to meet you. Your son proved to be invaluable on this trip." Brenley shook hands with both of them and smiled. "Unfortunately, I must be going. Scout, we'll file those follow-up reports later."

"Yes, ma'am." Scout tried not to smile at her anxious departure. His parents frowned at the archeologist's back.

"She seems to be a strange one." His mother's mouth turned down briefly before she smiled at Scout.

"Academics lack the common sense of business people. Always lost in their heads." His dad shrugged and started walking. "Let's get home. I have to make a noon meeting."

Scout's recounting of the trip didn't even take the entire drive home. There was little to share without mentioning blood or time travelers. His dad left immediately for his meeting and his mom closed herself up in her office.

With Maya curled up next to him, Scout went to sleep despite the mid-morning hour. A dreamless sleep lasted until his mom knocked on his door for dinner. He checked in with Brenley, showered, and then had a family meal.

Restless, he told his parents he was meeting Leyna and took off with Maya. He drove to the same overlook they'd visited together. He hadn't planned to bring the artifacts, but they were still in his bag.

Scout set them on the ground in front of him and Maya. He started with the black Jaguar and lightly touched it. Its warmth was comforting. The green Turtle felt cool and invigorating when he held it. It took an effort to put it down and turn to the final one. The Snake stared up at him as if in challenge. He took a deep breath and picked it up.

A burst of energy rippled through him, but the scene before his eyes didn't change. Scout released his breath and smiled. That was when he saw Dacey appear.

"I thought you might try this."

"You saved my life." Scout clutched the Snake tighter and tried to say more.

"You don't have to hold it. The power is connected to you a little more each time. It will become more familiar like the Jaguar and the Turtle already have."

Trusting the man, Scout placed it down and glanced up quickly. Dacey grinned at him then laughed.

"What are the images I see?"

No longer laughing, Dacey looked out at the horizon. "I do not know what you see."

"But you know why I see it? You had the Turtle, you're obsessed with all things Mayan. There's got to be more you can tell me."

Dacey dropped to the ground in a cross-legged position without making a sound. "I know you need to have all of the artifacts and you need to protect them."

"I'm calling bull on that. How are you even here? I don't think I'm dreaming and you said you weren't a ghost. You move through time and space like a Traveler, but no one seems to know about you. There's a lot you aren't telling me."

"Why are you looking for the artifacts?" Dacey sat absolutely still and stared at Scout.

Fidgeting, Scout patted Maya's head and looked around. "Okay, I'll play along. I started searching to prove to myself I wasn't crazy. Now…" It was harder to share the truth than he'd expected. The pull toward the artifacts continued to grow. "I don't want anyone to use them to destroy the world. Isn't the whole 'save the universe' excuse good enough?"

"Once upon a time, I made the same choice to save the universe. I was told you would come for the Turtle, and that it was my job to help you—"

"This is you helping me? Really?" Scout stood and glared at the man still sitting calmly. "If you want to help me, tell me what the hell is going on!"

Dacey stood and nodded once. "You know the basics. The orb was used to create your artifacts. The power was to be used to protect and serve the Mayas, but there was no balance. Families claimed the sculptures and separated the energy."

Scout felt the man was looking through him. He didn't breathe for fear of interrupting him.

"Instead of unity, there was only destruction. Brothers fought brothers. Blood, death, and loss. Fire and water. Night and day. Only the tree remained, but it was not enough to save the people." Dacey blinked and a small smile slowly graced his face. "Time is a strange and wondrous thing. This time can be different. You must keep the power together so it cannot be a weapon of destruction."

"How exactly am I supposed to do that?" Scout felt energy flowing around them. He could almost see the waves rippling through the forest.

Dacey again sat on the ground with his arms resting on his bent legs. "You become the Guardian, a warrior. You channel the power through you so only you can use it. Balanced, unified, and steady, you must stand firm in the center. If you fail…"

"It kills me and the whole world is destroyed. That part I get. What I don't understand is how to stop that from happening. I've seen enough people die. I don't want to be responsible for more deaths." Scout kicked a fallen branch and watched it sail through the air. "If you really want to help me, tell me what to do."

He felt the familiar flash of heat, but it was quickly extinguished by a cool breeze. The ripples surrounding them grew larger before calming. A sense of calm stole over him until his heart rate was slow, slower than normal.

"Are you doing that?"

Dacey's mouth quirked up before he laughed. "I have learned some tricks over the years."

Scout wanted to ask more about the tricks, but knew he needed to focus on his job. "Can you tell me what to do? Show me how to be a Guardian?"

"I can't." Dacey offered no apology or comfort. "You are the Guardian. I am only a messenger who can continue to guide you, but the choices must be yours. It begins and ends with you. Look inside yourself for the truth and the power of a warrior's sacrifice."

Before Scout could curse or scream at the vague words, his phone rang and Brenley's image popped up on the screen.

"She brings you wisdom, but the choices remain yours."

The phone buzzed again, Maya barked, and Dacey disappeared.

"Perfect timing, Doc."

"You are being sarcastic, but I do have important information." Her tone was as sharp as his had been.

Scout scratched Maya's ears and looked at the artifacts still laid out in front of him. He wasn't feeling quite as calm, but there was no fire or ice bringing pain and fear. "I have some information for you too, but I'm not ready to share it yet. You first."

She issued a soft sigh. "I've been researching the painting Hugo showed us. The one from the El Mirador cenote that looked like the parchment you have." Brenley's next words came out in a rush. "I think there's something missing, and what's not there is very important."

Scout settled more comfortably with his back against a tree and Maya crawled onto his lap. "Missing from the painting or the original drawing in the cenote?"

"Both, actually. I called in a favor and have spoken to the team of researchers there now. They thought my request was strange, but that is another term that's relative. I'm getting off-topic." She stuttered to a stop and took several deep breaths.

"Is this another sleep-deprived leap forward in our research?" Scout let his gaze wander around the forest. The waves of energy had disappeared with Dacey. It was surprisingly silent considering the current warm spell as spring approached. The hint of pine teased his senses and allowed him to relax.

"The parchment has the symbol for zero in the middle of the compass. It was that symbol Dacey used in his painting to represent you."

"Yes, I remember that part. Are you saying the painting doesn't have that symbol?" Scout's hand hovered over the Snake, but he didn't pick it up. Dacey's words repeated in his mind – balance and unity, truth and power, a warrior's sacrifice, only a messenger. Until he had the fourth artifact, Scout couldn't find balance. He wasn't sure he wanted power.

The sounds of Brenley typing filled the silence until she responded. "There's only a black circle in the center. I asked about Hugo when I called the museum. He is doing fine and has no memory of the attack. The museum received a report from the FBI that it was an attempt to stop our visit. They have reported several pieces were stolen."

"As the FBI hasn't visited me again, I assume you and I are in the clear."

"It is never smart to assume, Scout. I asked and was told we may be questioned as witnesses. They believe it is an existing ring of thieves covering their tracks." Brenley took a deep breath then another. "I asked the onsite team to X-ray the cenote drawing. I want to see if there is something beneath the black."

"And if there is, what does that tell us?" Her silence

made him groan. "You don't know yet and you don't want to speculate either. Is that all you wanted to talk about?"

"I wanted to make sure you were okay. As I'm still in Virginia, we can meet in person. Maybe you'll feel more like telling me the truth if we are talking face to face." The small sniff revealed her annoyance.

Scout laughed and nodded to himself. "Yes, that's probably a good idea." He again looked at the three pieces. "Brenley, can I ask you something?"

"Of course."

"What do you think is happening when I touch the artifacts? I mean, are the visions real? Is it really distorting time or is that just in my head?" He forced his hands to open and pat Maya instead of clutching her to his chest. The silence wasn't as long as he'd expected or feared.

"I don't know, Scout, but I'm looking for the truth. If it is a future technology used in the past...that's not something I've heard of or studied."

He nodded even though she couldn't see it. "Yeah, I get that. It's not fair to expect you to have all the answers."

"There is something I know." There was a smile in her tone. "I know you are a warrior. You are strong, brave, and loyal. If anyone can do this, it's you. I told you – you are the one I trust."

"You are a strange one, Doc." He chuckled nervously then blew out a quick breath. "And I'm glad you are. You're the only one still standing by me. That means a lot."

"Scout, we have both lied. You should talk to Leyna—"

"I didn't jump to conclusions. She confirmed she had

lied." Scout rolled his shoulders back and waited for her to argue.

"Okay. The decision is yours to make."

Dacey's words echoed in Scout's mind. '...*the choices must be yours. It begins and ends with you.*' The images of the four warriors flashed as the words repeated. Yellow – Blue – Red –White. Body paint and feathers. Spears, bows, and ropes. Darkness.

"Scout, I've just heard back from the research team."

Jerking back to reality, Scout processed her words. "Okay, is there anything behind the black?"

"There is – it's an image of a bat."

"Like the animal?"

"Yes, of course," Brenley snapped. She sighed then took several breaths. When she spoke again, her tone was soft. "There's a bat in the middle of the Jaguar, Turtle, Snake, and Owl."

Scout studied the artifacts in front of him as she named them off. He waited several seconds before rolling his eyes. "I know you don't want to guess, but what did the bat symbolize for the Mayans?"

"The bat is associated with night, death, and sacrifice."

"That fits in with everything else so far." Scout stood and lightly struck a tree with his free hand. "I guess that tells us what happens if we fail."

More images burned in his head – jungles and beaches – pyramids and cenotes – blood, always blood.

"I think it tells us more than that." Brenley's hushed voice was almost reverent.

"What do you think it means then?" Scout packed up the artifacts and stowed them in his bag. He fully expected the archeologist to refuse to share her untested theories.

"I think it means there's a fifth artifact."

At her words, a new image invaded his thoughts. The dark sky was ripped open by flashes of yellow, blue, red, and white. The flap of wings grew louder behind the snake descending the pyramid. A shadow separated from the serpent and flew through the pale blue sky. It merged with the only tree growing on the beach. Dark lines spilled from the tree to surround it before burrowing in the sand. Its limbs extended into the sky as it darkened into night once again. One red line split the sky in two – Orion on one side, the Pleaides on the other.

...the choices must be yours. It begins and ends with you. Look inside yourself for the truth and the power of a warrior's sacrifice.

A blinding white light flashed and the ground shook under Scout. His hands scraped along the tree trunk as he pulled himself up to stand. The Virginia forest again surrounded him as Maya barked at his feet.

"...I mean, I'm not sure. We'll need to research this as it could be a personal message from Dacey. But if there is a fifth artifact—"

"The Bat is the fifth artifact, and we have to find it before anyone else does."

Rennie St. James loves to put a fictional spin on her favorite things. Adopted kittens transform into mountain lions and jaguars. Martial arts training creates powerful modern warriors. Chocolate is delicious and healthy! Her fantasy books include all of these things plus a bit of travel, magic, and romance. In addition to the Atlantic Island Universe: Guardian trilogy, the first five books of her debut urban fantasy series, the Rahki Chronicles, are available now. Rennie also has drabbles and short stories included in several multi-author anthologies released in 2019. You can find her all over social media as she loves to interact with fellow bookworms and authors.

Website: https://writerrsj.com/

ABOUT FREDRIC

Fredric Shernoff is the author of the Atlantic Island Universe, including the Amazon Top 100 "Atlantic Island" and the Barnes and Noble #1 bestseller "The Traveler."

Fredric lives in Palm Beach Gardens, Florida with his wife and best friend, Cheslie, and their three amazing children.

Join the mailing list at fredricshernoff.com to stay up to date on new releases!

facebook.com/fredricshernoffauthor

amazon.com/author/fredricshernoff

bookbub.com/authors/Fredric-shernoff

Mosaics by Dawn Dagger

Fragments of Time (Book 1)

Fractures in Stars (Book 2) - July, 2020

Odyssey by Skylar Jaymes (AJ Kurtz)

Marked by Fate (Book 1)

Bound by Fate (Book 2) - August, 2020

Destiny by LaLa Leo

Genesis (Book 1)

Revelation (Book 2) - October, 2020